BLACK REIGN

Also by
Edd McNair

My Time to Shine

BLACK REIGN

EDD MCNAIR

www.urbanbooks.net

Urban Books
1199 Straight Path
West Babylon, NY 11704

ISBN 1-60162-133-7

Second Printing January 2008
Printed in the Canada

10 9 8 7 6 5 4 3 2

BLACK REIGN

PART I

ANGELA

Chapter One

"Hurry up, Angah," Angela's little brother yelled, unable to pronounce her name. "Mommy said, 'Hurry up now.'" He tried to annoy her.

"Shut up, boy. I'm glad I'm graduating today, so I can get the hell out of here."

"You're not out of here yet, so I would watch my mouth if I were you," her mother replied from down the stairs, surprising Angela, who thought she was outside by the car.

Angela had been the only child up to five years ago. Her parents had divorced when she was ten. Her father, a licensed electrician, had provided a comfortable life for her and her mother. Her mother got pregnant with her in high school, which made things difficult, but with the help of grandparents, she was still able to attend Old Dominion University and receive her nursing degree.

Together they worked hard to move themselves into Virginia Beach's only upper-class, all-black neighborhood, L & J Gardens, where they purchased their first two-story, three-bedroom, contemporary-style home. They felt at the time that being around other black folks who had what they had was going to classify them as "better" black folks.

As her mother left for Leigh Memorial every morning and her father for whatever he did, Angela thought to herself, *They have the perfect marriage.* Until one day she came home and all her father's things were gone. He realized that family life wasn't for him—five years after the fact—but kept on paying the mortgage, so her mother never asked for anything else.

Angela resented him for a long time, but now she was older and had learned to look at the situation from another angle. Her mother and father argued all the time, and many times she could see why her father left, but didn't dare say that to her moms. Her father always kept in touch, and she spent summers with him in Beltsville, Maryland.

After two years of being alone and trying the dating scene, Angela's mother met Dr. Statton, or Ken, which he told her to call him. Ken didn't look as good as Angela's father, but he treated her mother well. Angela remembers the trips and the long weekends Ken and her moms would take. (She would be left at her grandparent's house.)

It wasn't long before Angela's mother was pregnant with her little brother. They never married, but Ken was always in the picture. Angela admired the way Ken treated her mother and promised that any man she would even consider marrying would have to do the same.

* * *

As they traveled to her graduation, Angela was so excited about starting college in the fall, and that her parents had agreed to give her a hand if she got her own place closer to campus. If they didn't, she was going to stay on campus—no way in hell was she going to stay home and have her moms all up in her business. Most of her friends would be going to school out of state, but she and her best friend, Monica, had decided to go to Hampton University.

When they arrived at graduation, Monica was waiting for her at the door. The girls took off so they could get with their classmates. Angela was talking to Monica when someone grabbed her from behind. She turned around to see her boyfriend Ray standing there.

"You still goin' to Allen pool party after graduation? His parents suppose to be out of town, so it got to be the hype shit." Ray shook his head to confirm that what he was saying was the truth.

Angela looked at Monica. "Monica, are we going to Allen party?"

"Yeah, but we goin' to get there later on because we got to stop at Ski shit first—he havin' his party out Lake Edward at the clubhouse. And you know how them LE niggahs roll." Monica gave Angela a high five, knowing it would irk Ray. "Heah, Ray," Monica said, "you comin' to Ski party?"

"I don't know—I ain't for the bullshit tonight. I'll probably just see y'all at Allen house later. That Lake Edward shit probably end early anyway . . . guaranteed."

* * *

Ray grew up in Wesleyan Chase, not too far from L & J Gardens, but just down the street from Lake Edward apartments, which was known for drugs, violence, and other illegal activities. Ray hadn't planned on going to college. Actually he never cared too much for school; he knew he was going to work for his dad and one day take over the business, Decker and Sons Plumbing.

Ray stood about 5' 10" and weighed about 210 pounds solid, which kept him destroying kids on the wrestling mat. He ultimately became captain of the wrestling team and two-time state champion contender. Ray had been with Angela since the summer before their junior year. He was popular among his peers and somebody the young ladies would kill to be with, but he knew Angela was no one to give any space to. Any man would gladly scoop her up with the quickness. Her dazzling light-brown eyes, smooth golden-brown skin, full and beautifully shaped lips, perfectly shaped ass that stunned men, no matter what she wore, all packed in a size eight frame with well-proportioned breasts. When the bra fell, the breasts didn't; they stood up and begged for attention. She was set off with a short Halle Berry cut, which made her an extraordinary package.

To top it off, she carried a 4.0 GPA. Even though there were equally attractive girls at Bayside H.S., Angela was the only girl for him. He loved her more than anything, and if it went his way, right after she finished school, they would be married.

As Angela sat in the stands listening to her principal speak, she then realized the day she never thought would come was here. She had everything planned; this summer she would work full-time as a receptionist. She had been there since the beginning of her senior year and really enjoyed it. Her and Monica were going to sign their lease at their new condo on the first of July, and then she'd be considered grown. The graduation class standing brought her back to reality as she heard the words, "Congratulations, class of 1996."

As they strolled out the stands, she made her way over to her father. She knew he would come. He never had anymore kids, and he always let her know that even though he was in Maryland and she in Virginia, she was the most important thing in his life. And he did a great job showing it, even if he wasn't local.

"Congratulations, baby girl," her father said as they embraced.

"Heah, Daddy." Angela smiled a wide smile, one that you could only get when in daddy's arms.

"Just because you out of school, don't mean shit—you ain't grown, goddamn!"

"Shut up, James," Lenore said. "I'm happy for you, love. Don't pay your dad any attention."

Lenore was from Washington, DC. Angela's father had met her about five years ago, and they had been living together about four years. In the beginning Angela didn't care too much for Lenore, but her father begged her to give her a chance— Angela's problem was that her father was almost forty and Lenore was twenty-eight. By the end of the summer, they were the best of friends.

Lenore was stern like her mother ... except,

hanging out with Lenore was fun. She was beautiful and, at the same time, fly as hell. She was a cosmetologist and had been doing hair since the tender age of twelve. By the time she was twenty, she had landed a job at one of the top salons in the Northern Virginia/DC area. Her appearance was always together—hair perfect, eyebrows arched, makeup applied as if it was professionally done, and a body to kill for. Over the years, Angela started to admire Lenore's style and wanted to be more like her than her mother.

Angela's mother never noticed that she was turning into a woman. She didn't want her to wear makeup, she wouldn't let her arch her eyebrows, and the thought of getting nails was totally out of the question. Angela always wore her hair long since she was a young girl, something her mother took great pride in. But last summer when she was in Maryland, Lenore was wearing a short cut that made her jealous. Angela cut hers in the same style without thinking twice. When she got back home, her mother was pissed, and she remembers her mom and dad on the phone arguing for what seemed like hours. Her mom promised her father that Angela would never spend another summer in Maryland again. Her father laughed, knowing this was the last summer before Angela graduated, and her mother wouldn't have shit else to say about that situation.

"So what you doin' tonight?" Lenore handed Angela a card.

"Me and Monica goin' to a couple parties, that's it." Angela responded as if it was nothing.

"Be safe, and no drinking and driving out here," Lenore said.

"Here come your grandparents, baby. We'll be here until Sunday at the Sheraton downtown Waterside. The room is under my name. Call me." James leaned over and kissed his daughter again.

"Hello, James," her grandparents said.

"Hello." James turned to Angela. "Call me," he said as he strolled off.

Angela's mother came up and hugged her. She held her face, looked into her eyes, and told her how proud she was and from here on nothing could hold her back. Her eyes began to water. "Don't cry, Ma," Angela said, trying not to get emotional.

"Baby, we're all just so proud of you," her grandmother said.

Just then, Dr. Statton walked up, holding her little brother. "Congratulations, love," he said, hugging her.

Angela reached up and hugged him real tight. Even though he had never married her mother, he had been there through some tough times. Through her teenage years, many times she felt her mother didn't understand what she was going through, but Dr. Statton did, and he would come to her rescue. Many nights when her mother worked, Dr. Statton would be at the house to cook, clean, and take care of her and her brother. She referred to him as her step-dad to her friends, and even though he never told her, he was like putty in her hands. He couldn't love her anymore if she was his own.

"Thank you, Ken."

"I forgot your gift, but you'll get it tomorrow. And just because you out of school, don't forget your curfew."

"Ken," Angela said in a whining voice.

"Okay"—he smiled—"you have an extra hour."

Angela smiled and her mother just stared.

They all began walking to the car when Monica and Ray came up, "Hello, Ms. Wood, Dr. Statton," Ray said.

"Hello, Raymond," her mother replied.

"Girl, what you gonna do?" Monica asked.

"Ain't nothin' change. I'll be at the house waiting on you. Don't you have to change?"

"Yeah, I was just asking. I'll see you in a few." Monica said, and she and Ray walked off.

Angela was trying to figure out what to wear. She didn't know if she was going to swim or what. She called Monica to see what was up. "Heah, what you puttin' on?"

"Shorts and a T-shirt," Monica said. "Bitches might be tryin' to act up tonight, and I ain't for it."

"I'll throw my suit on under my other shit."

"Just hurry the fuck up, girl. I'll see you in five."

Angela pulled her white, two-piece body glove swimsuit out her drawer along with her sleeveless button-down that tied in the front. It was a little wrinkled, but she knew it would come off as soon as she got up the street. She twisted into her new Levi shorts, stepped back and looked into the mirror at how the jeans fit real snug on her phat ass, and let out a satisfying smile.

Just then the door to her room flew open. "Hurry up, bitch, we got some stops to make."

"Where?" Angela reached into her closet for her new white Reebok Classics.

"You'll see, come on."

Angela loved her buddy, but she knew at times she had to calm her down. She and Monica had been friends since grade school. (Monica's parents were killed in an accident when she was seven, leaving her and her brother of nine to be raised by her grandparents, who lived in L & J Gardens. Soon after, she met Angela, and they've been hanging ever since.)

"Girl, you know them shorts screamin'," Monica said.

"They'll make the niggahs scream more. And look at your shit."

"Shut your mouth—I'm grown now."

They both began to laugh.

Angela was fine and she knew it, but Monica was no slouch. Monica was light skinned and stood a little taller than Angela at about 5' 5". Her ass wasn't as phat as Angela's, but it stuck out farther. Her breasts were bigger, with large nipples that usually poked through her blouse. When she was younger, it bothered her; now it was an attention-getter, and she knew how to handle it. She would always catch guys staring right at them. Her hair, lightened almost to a gold to complement her complexion, hung down on her shoulders, with little spiral curls all over. She wasn't conceited but she knew that her narrow nose, small lips, high cheekbones, slanted eyes, and grey pupils that changed colors with the sun would fuck any niggah's head up.

Chapter Two

Monica and Angela jumped in the car, headed to Ski's party. Before they could hit Baker Road, they had their shirts off and had thrown them in the back seat.

"Where do we have to stop?" Angela asked.

"Goin' out St. Croix and see what Fat Joe and Rome up to. They told me to stop by. Rome said I could come by—if I brought you."

"See, you tryin' to start somethin'. Suppose somebody else is over there and go to Allen party and tell Ray. Then I'm in some shit, and God knows I'm not tryin' to lose my man, Monica."

"It ain't even like that. We just goin' over there and smoke their weed, and then we out."

"You know Ski got weed—fuck them niggahs. You just want to see Joe fat ass. I don't see what you see in him anyway."

"He's not bad lookin'—he got good hair, he dress his ass off, and he keeps weed."

"His *momma* keep weed," Angela said, correcting her.

"Don't matter. She don't care. And plus, he's sweet."

"Why you fuck that fat muthafucka anyway?"

"Because we friends like that, and he never runs his mouth. We've been friends like that since eleventh grade. I was going over there everyday after school smoking weed, and he would always hint around. Then one day I was playing with him, and he just started licking my pussy, girl, and I was hooked. He's not a bad lover. Better try you a fat, muthafuckin'-ass niggah."

"It's all right; I'll leave them to you. What about Quinn?" Angela asked.

"That's my baby. But by him livin' in Petersburg attendin' Virginia State, that long-distance shit gets hard, and Fat Joe is cool . . . my fat man." They both burst out laughing.

Monica had been with her share of guys, what some people would consider fast. She had gone to private school up to the ninth grade, but when she got to Bayside, she got wide open. By her junior year, she had calmed down and decided to only be with Quinn. Fat Joe was just her friend then.

Angela, on the other hand, had lost her virginity at fourteen to Monica's brother. (He was real light like Monica and had grey eyes. Girls were always crazy about him.) One weekend she stayed with Monica. He came in their room and, with their grandmother in the next room, took her virginity. She remembers the first couple times it hurt, but as it became more frequent she came to enjoy it. When Angela realized that she was just a

toy to him, she stopped giving in to his secret plea-
sures.

She then started talking to Ski, well known and
real popular, not only at Bayside, but also throughout the Tidewater area. Ski was the high-school
starting running back and was shown many Friday
nights on the news, scoring touchdowns and doing
interviews. He held city records in track and was
what people consider a track star. Not even a
month into their relationship, he had girls from
Green Run, Norview, and Booker T. all wanting to
fight her over him. She got tired of fighting
bitches for no reason, so she let him go and vowed
she would never talk to any one like him again.

Then Ray came along. Very popular amongst
the students at Bayside because of his wrestling
skills and his muscular body; he was laid back and
quiet. He was never about trouble but could hold
his own. He was so sweet to her, always having sweet
things to say, giving her rides to and from school,
when Monica didn't. They just clicked from the
beginning and it's been love ever since. Angela
had no real desire to be with any other guy. Ray
was her love; the only love she would ever need.

"Look, girl, there's Dirt-Dirt car," Angela said.

"He fixed his little Escort up." Monica laughed.
"I bet you anything Tammy and Ki over here."

"Shit, I know them bitches here. There's their
momma car over there—Goddamn, girl," Angela
said all excited, as if she was about to jump out her
seat, "whose burgundy Lexus with the thirty-day
tags?"

"Girl, that's Rome shit."

"He traded in the Honda? What he doin'?" Angela asked.

"Naw, he gettin' it fixed; it's in the shop. You know he be drivin' his brother cars."

"Who's his brother?"

"Bo," Monica answered.

Angela got out the car. "Who the hell is Bo?"

"You remember our sophomore year when they had that big drug bust, and those Lake Edward niggahs got caught up?"

Angela gave Monica a dazed look.

"Remember that sports bar that was up by the Food Lion where all those hustlers use to hang out?"

"Yeah," Angela said, "we were like fifteen, sixteen years old."

"Well, the head niggah name was Black. I never met him, I just heard about him. But you know Lo from out Lake Edward, right?"

Angela asked, "Didn't he get like fifteen years or somethin'?"

"Yeah, that's him, but word is, he suppose to be comin' home soon and shit will hit the fan. They say that when they got busted, Bo told everything to save his own ass and didn't do six months. Bo use to run hand in hand with them, and after shit went down, Bo hit the street and kept his own shit goin'. That's why he gettin' it now."

"Shit, he ain't doin' all that," Angela said, "because my cousin Quandra use to fuck with Lo, and she said that niggah was rich. I mean a-new-car-every-six-months rich."

"Well, he makin' money and he looks out for

Rome. That's why Rome always dressed his ass off. You like that Lexus though, don't you?"

"Yeah, I do." Angela knocked on the door.

Fat Joe answered the door with a blunt in his hand. The house had about ten people inside, and the room was full of smoke.

"Where's your moms?" Monica asked.

"She had to work all night; it's my spot tonight. Why? What's up?"

"Nothin', fool." Monica made her way through the crowd and to the couch.

"Wannabe, hood rats in this bitch," Rome yelled.

"If they ain't fuckin', tell them to carry they ass home," Dirt-Dirt yelled. "Talk to me, Rome."

Rome grabbed his dick. "All these bitches know my steez, son."

"Why y'all so fuckin' nasty?" Monica asked.

"I wa'n' talkin' to you; she know who I'm screamin' at."

Angela said, "I ain't playin' with you, Rome."

"I ain't *playin'*."

"Leave her alone, Rome," Fat Joe said, "before I call Ray around this bitch."

Rome jumped up. "Ray who? Must mean Ray Mercer, the heavyweight niggah . . . because that's who you'll need to pull me out his ass."

Everyone started laughing.

"Niggahs must not know where the fuck I'm from." Rome gave the crowd the LE holler, and everyone responded. Then he sat, passed Angela the blunt, and slid closer to her. "So you goin' to Hampton, huh?"

"Yeah, everything already set."

"I'll be over there with you."

"For real?" Angela was excited. Just the thought of somebody else from school going over there made her feel good.

"I got to go; all the bitches over there. I'm goin' hang with you and Monica and fuck all your friends."

"You got problems, boy," Angela said to Rome.

"You ain't goin' look out, Angela?"

"Hell no, that's fuckin' triflin'."

"I'm goin' look out, Rome." Monica got up and gave him a pound. "Put you in there with all those stupid-ass 'ho's. Now pass that L."

"I heard that. See, Monica my girl; Angela be on some bullshit."

They sat around drinking, smoking trees, and listening to the latest sounds being played by the 103 JAMZ. After talking about anybody and every-body—who didn't graduate or who wasn't going to college—Fat Joe finally realized the time and thought it was time to burst, so he began to clean up.

Everybody headed out the door except for Monica and Angela. Knowing how his mother was, they didn't want him to catch hell later on. She didn't mind the drinking, smoking, or the com-pany, as long as her shit was clean when she came home.

Rome came back through the door. "Last chance, Angela—What's up?" He threw his hands up.

"I'm okay, Rome." Angela smiled. "Thanks any-way."

Rome picked up his keys off the table. "Rollin' with me, Fats, or you drivin'?"

"I'm rollin' in the Lex, muthafucka. What the

hell I look like? I want to shine for the bitches a little bit too." Fats held the door for them to get out.

They arrived at the clubhouse about eleven
o'clock. It was packed inside and out, young 'uns
all up and down Lake Edward Drive, hanging in the
streets, acting up. Monica and Angela parked the
car and headed to the clubhouse.

The kid at the door had a stern look. "Five dollars a head for everybody—no exceptions."

"Tell Ski Angela out here, fool," Monica said,
knowing Ski would look out for Angela.

Ski came to the door. "Monica, your charge is a
hug." Ski reached out and hugged her real rough,
in a playful manner. "Angela, your charge is a big-
ass hug and at least one dance. Slow dance. One
where I can get my freak on." He pulled her real
close and tight, and hugged her, then let out a satisfying smile.

"We'll see. You know what's up" Angela said.

"Ray my man; he won't mind." Ski led them into
the party.

They weren't in the party twenty minutes before
Angela was ready to go. When she wasn't high, she
didn't worry too much, but as soon as she got her
smoke on, she became very observant and eventually paranoid if not in a calm environment. (She
first tried weed her sophomore year and realized
she liked the feeling of being high. She found herself giggling and smiling about everything—that's
how her mother and Ken would know she'd been
smoking.)

She went and found Monica who was in the corner smoking with Fat Joe and Rome, and gave her
a look to let her know she was ready to go. Monica

didn't mind because she was anxious to see who
was at Allen's party anyway.

By the time she arrived at Allen's party she knew
her time was limited. Allen's party she could enjoy—
it was laid back and she knew nothing was going to
kick off unexpected. Angela enjoyed hanging with
the other crowd, but at times they could really get
out of hand. Their idea of a good party was only if
the party ended with niggahs fighting or a little
gunplay.

Allen's parents lived in Church Point, an exclusive neighborhood not too far from the high
school they all attended. His father was an electri-
cal engineer, and his mother was an architect.
Together they made his life quite comfortable in
their eight-hundred-thousand-dollar home. They
allowed him to have his pool party, but he was
warned that it could not get out of hand under any
circumstances.

When Monica and Angela walked in the back,
all eyes fell on them. They looked extremely sexy in
their shorts and bathing suit tops. All their classmates came up and started mingling, except for
those in the pool. Before she realized Ray was behind her, he scooped her up and took her to the
edge of the pool like he was going to throw her in.
She begged him not to drop her, but she saw in his
eyes that it was about to happen and changed her
tactics. Instead of trying to resist, she reached out
and hugged him, and in a soft whisper said,
"Please let me take off these shorts and sneakers
and I'll get in with you."

He agreed instantly. "You promise?"

Nothing and no one was as sexy as his girl to

him. He watched her as she walked over and took off her shorts and sneakers. He gently took her hand and guided her into the pool with him. His day was going well. If she hadn't showed up, it would have devastated him.

"What took y'all so long?"

She looked into his eyes. She loved when he expressed himself and asked her questions, like what she did was so important. She stood there as he held her, splashing water. She felt like a child having the time of her life.

After spending a half hour in the pool playing around, he eased up behind her. "Can we go?" he asked softly in her ear. "I know you have to be home soon and I just want some private time with my girl. Just you and me."

"Yes," she said smiling. She was really ready to go when he first picked her up. She felt her body aching for his touch, and all she wanted was to lay down, enjoy her high, and let him have his way.

"Heah, Monica," Angela yelled, "I'm gettin' outta here. I'll call you tomorrow."

Angela sat in the car thinking, while Ray went inside the Cricket Inn to get a room. *Why would he pay for a room and I only had a little over an hour to be home?*

He jumped in the car all smiles. "I know we don't have much time, but I didn't want to go somewhere and sneak like we've done so many times before. I want to take my time and enjoy you."

She sat excited like a child, feeling good about what he was feeling. They went inside the room. Without hesitation they began to undress slowly, looking at each other as if not to be the first to undress.

They climbed into bed. He began kissing her as if there was no tomorrow. She was overwhelmed and responded immediately. He lifted up, put on a condom, and positioned himself between her legs. She lay back, stared into his eyes, and lifted her legs up and back to accept him. He slowly eased his way inside of her and felt the moistness from her body—it quickly let him know that he wasn't going to last long.

She laid there not moving, just holding him tight as he bucked hard and fast like the young stud he was. She was starting to feel so good when she felt his body tense up and began to jolt. She tried to hold him, but he jumped up and hurried to the shower.

She was enjoying herself so much. She wanted him in her arms, to make love to her again. She got out of bed and went inside the bathroom figuring she would get in the shower and get him excited again. She pulled back the shower curtain and noticed his masculine body dripping with soap and water. She looked down at his thick, short penis swinging. *Just moments ago it stood up, stiff as a board.* She climbed in and stood behind him. She rubbed his back, then his chest. As she reached down to touch his penis, he turned around, rinsed the soap off his back, gave her a kiss, and jumped out. She stood there letting the shower drown her frustrations. She wanted him so bad, and he was done. When Angela finished showering, Ray took her home.

"I'll see you tomorrow," she said.

"In the evening, I got to help my father with something early. I'll call you when I finish, okay. I love you, Angela."

She pushed the car door open. He grabbed her arm, leaned over, and gave her a kiss. Again she was smiling inside.

Chapter Three

The following morning Angela woke up to the smell of breakfast cooking. It wasn't too often her mom got up before eleven on Saturday. *Why was today special?*

She wiped the cold from her eyes as she strolled to the kitchen. "Ma, why you up so early?"

"It's nine and it's not early. And I'm not your mother," Ken said. "I'm making breakfast. I need just a few more minutes. So if you get showered and dressed, we'll go shopping before anyone else gets up."

Shopping was all she needed to hear. Within minutes she had showered and was coming out the room.

Her family was sitting at the kitchen table, eating. She sat down and joined them. As she ate, she wondered if Ken was still going to take her shopping.

Her mother handed her a card. "Look, here is your graduation gift from Ken and I."

"Will you get my checkbook out my car right quick for me, Angela," Ken said. "I'll write you a check, but I'm not going to have time to go to the mall; you may have to call Monica."

"If I had my own car I wouldn't have to call nobody."

Angela opened the door and let out a scream. Ken stood there with the keys to a brand-new '96 Jetta. Angela knew this was Dr. Statton's doing. After looking in the car, around the car, she stood back and smiled as she opened her card. Five crispy hundred-dollar bills fell out. She ran over and gave Ken the biggest hug he had ever gotten. "Thank you, Ken. Thank you, Mom. I love you guys so much." Angela's eyes filled with tears of joy.

Ken felt so good to be able to give her something , and for her to appreciate it like she did . . . "Listen to me, Angela, we bought you this car so you can get to work and back and forth to school— that was our sole purpose. The payments are three hundred and sixty-eight dollars a month, the insurance is seventy-seven dollars a month. Can you afford that and the rent you're about to get into?"

"I can now, if I'm full-time, but not when school start."

"You work for me now. Your job is to go to school like you're supposed to and bring grades home to my satisfaction, and I'll pay your note and insurance. But if the grades fall or if they aren't up to par, you will quit the receptionist job, you will move back on campus, and I'll sell your car to one of my interns. Do you understand?"

"Yes, sir. I understand, sir." Angela shook Ken's hand and laughed.

She ran to the phone to call Monica. "Get up, girl. I got a car and some money, and I'm headed to Lynnhaven Mall. See you in ten minutes." She jetted out the door, happier than any eighteen-year-old could ever imagine herself to be. She thought that now she could get around, take care of the things she needed to do without worrying anyone. She wouldn't have any problem getting back and forth to work or to and from school in the fall. And now she could even drive when her and Ray went out. That excuse, "I don't feel like picking you up and then carrying you back home," was out the window. *July couldn't get here fast enough*, Angela thought. She called Ray from Monica's house to share the good news.

Ray seemed happy for her, but didn't share the same excitement. His responsibilities as her boy-friend were about to be cut down. He enjoyed pick-ing her up from work after practice and picking her up and going out. Most of all he enjoyed her depending on him and being there for her—this was his way of keeping her under his wing. Now it was going to be just conversations here and there as she ran and handled her own business. He would no longer be able to keep tabs on her, and this worried him. He knew she wouldn't betray him and he trusted her. But he knew his girl was fine—she had a beautiful body, she carried her-self like a mature woman and any man would be more than happy to take her. That's who he didn't trust.

*   *   *

Angela was finally moving into her new condo. (Ken knew a doctor who had purchased a condo in Willoughby, a beautiful section of Norfolk. The doctor moved to Virginia Beach and decided to rent it out. Ken found it to be perfect. *She could get to school or her job within ten minutes*, he thought.) Monica was moving with her and had plenty of help. She was inside chilling when Ray came through the door, then Angela and her help. "Heah, girlfriend. Heah, Ray."

"What's up, girl? What's up, Quinn, Rome," Angela said. "Can I get some help bringin' my shit in—all these hard-head muthafuckas standing around."

Monica's brother came out of her room, catching Angela by surprise. "What's up, Angie?"

Angela gave him a hug. *Smell good*, she thought, *and still fine as hell, if not finer, but never again.* "Monica's breakin' the lease already—they said no pets—especially no dogs in this bitch."

He stood staring her up and down and smiling, figuring maybe he could be her friend, now that her and his sister was roommates. *God she filled out beautifully and has grown to be quite a woman.* "How you been? It's been a little while."

"I'm fine. Just fine."

"Let's grab your shit," Rome said walking out the door. "I got to run." Everybody followed.

Later on Monica and Quinn sat on the couch sipping Heinekens, while Angela and Ray got her room situated. They all started talking about what they were going to do for the Fourth of July.

"Turn that down a little bit," Ray said.

"You don't like Outkast, niggah?" Quinn asked.

"They be rockin'"—Angela said—"me and you, your momma, and your cousin too." They all started laughing, and that started a long conversation about hip-hop music.

As the night progressed, they grew tired and decided it was time to retire. "Let me go make my bed," Angela said. "I'm getting tired."

"For real, girl, I'm gonna go climb in my bed as soon as I take care of something." Monica pulled out a quarter of weed and a box of blunts.

"I heard that shit, girl."

"Roll up," Quinn said, getting some extra energy.

"Let me make my bed up real quick so all I have to do is jump in. Come on, Ray, you know I need your help." Angela picked up her bag from Wal-Mart to get her new sheets, pillows, and comforter as her and Ray began to make the bed.

"Why you have to smoke that shit?" Ray asked.

"Just because you don't smoke weed, don't knock my thing. Plus, it's only every now and then."

"Yeah, right. I bet it's gonna be an everyday thing now you have your own spot."

"No, it's not, Ray, but if I decide to, I have that right—I pay these bills around here."

"And I have the right to leave."

"Whatever." Angela kept making the bed. After she finished, she asked Ray, "Are you going to stay in the room or come out and chill?"

"If you're going to smoke, I'm going to head home."

She didn't want him to leave, but she wasn't going to argue or be controlled by anyone. Her father was in Maryland, maybe Ray forgot that.

"Will I see you tomorrow?" she asked as if she didn't mind. She sat on the couch as he went out the door.

"What's up with Ray, Angela?" Monica asked.

"Niggah trippin' . . . tellin' me I shouldn't smoke. He don't know I'm fuckin' grown." Then to Quinn, "Now pass the blunt, fool."

Quinn passed the blunt. "Y'all 'ho's crazy." Then he rolled another.

The summer seemed so short, Angela thought; *another week and school's going to be in session.* She sat on the couch flipping channels, feeling like life couldn't get any better. It was the weekend, and after the week she had, she was trying to enjoy doing nothing. Just then the phone rang.

"Hello."

"What's up, girl?" It was Monica.

"Nothin'. Just enjoyin' the day doin' nothin'."

"You want to go to Pizzazz tonight?"

"Where?"

"Granby Street," Monica said in an excited manner. "I want to check out that club Pizzazz, where the niggahs poppin' that Don and Crissy."

"I don't care; it really don't sound bad."

"I'll be home in a little bit."

Angela ran in the room to find something to

wear. *For the club, I have to have a little something, something to entice the fellows, and I really don't have shit.*

The ring of the phone disturbed her train of thought. She glanced at the caller ID to see it was Ray. She picked it up quickly. "Hello."

"What you doin'?"

"Nothin'. Just tryin' to find somethin' to wear."

"You comin' by to see me?"

"I've been running all week, Ray. I figured I would just relax. You can come by here for a little while."

"Okay, I'll see you later on."

"How later? Monica and I are goin' to the club later."

"Thought you were so tired. I'll give you a call tomorrow." Ray hung up.

"Hello . . . hello . . ."

Angela slammed down the phone. "I love that niggah, but he's starting to get on my mutha-fuckin' nerves—acting like a fuckin' bitch. If he was any kind of man, he'd be over here fuckin' the hell out of me, so I wouldn't have the energy to fuck with anybody else . . . instead of acting like a jealous kid."

She was mumbling now and tossing things around with a little more force than usual. Then she realized nobody was there. *I am not going to be worried, not today.* She continued to look for something to wear until she heard Monica come in.

"Got any company?" Monica yelled.

"Naw, girl, I'm chillin'."

"I hope you naked," Rome said loudly, " 'cause I'm comin' in." He walked into her room.

"What's up, Rome?"

"Ready to hit the club, find a little something, something."

"You look nice, Rome," Angela said.

"I know." Rome started pulling weed and a White Owl out of his pocket.

"Look at Rome, Angela," Monica said, "with his Calvin Klein gear, lookin' all good."

"Where did y'all hook up?" Angela asked.

"I was coming out of Hair Art, and he was going in Clippers, the barbershop next door. He started talking about going to Pizzazz, so I figured we all might swing out together and have a ball."

"So," Angela asked, "where you goin' to stay, Rome? On campus or what?"

"Naw, my brother got a spot in Hampton, so I'm gonna chill over there—rent-free, niggah."

"That shit worked out for ya, didn't it?" Monica put in Mobb Deep CD. She and Angela sat down as Rome lit the White Owl, knowing how slow it was going to burn. They knew the head would be right for the club.

"CD's are over there and some Heinekens are in the 'frigerator," Monica said to Rome as she walked to her room to get dressed.

"Hurry the hell up," Rome said real low and slow as if the weed was affecting him. "Don't be like my goddamn sister."

"Shut your high ass up, niggah," Angela said.

Rome reached in his pocket and pulled out a coin. "Heads, I wash Angela back; tails, I wash

Monica back—really, I don't give a fuck which one I clean." He smiled.

"Lock your door, Monica," Angela yelled out going into her room. "Niggah's bein' nasty."

Rome laughed so hard, he began choking. Then he sat down to finish the slow-burning White Owl.

Chapter Four

Rome pulled up in front of the club to check the crowd. The line was just down the building, so it was beginning to pack up. He cruised real slow past the crowd of people. He knew the two fine-ass bitches in the car made niggahs admire him, and the Lex made bitches want him. He felt like the man. He was so glad Bo was letting him drive it, but it was only for a minute, only while Bo was in the rough hanging on the corner trying to get. So for tonight he thought, *GS300 do your thing, do your thing*.

They parked and went inside the club, thinking about the fake ID's getting them over again. They thought the wait would be longer than it was, but the line moved pretty quickly. They eased to the third floor. Rome leaned over to the bar to order a drink.

"You not buyin' us a drink?" Angela asked.

"Just because I drive my brother's car don't mean I have his pocket." Rome had a smirk, like he was lying.

"We didn't ask you all that," Monica said.

"Is flat *no* better for ya? Just stand there and look pretty. Stick your ass out a little and y'all will have a drink in your hand in no time."

"Look what she got on."

"Look at that bitch head," Monica added.

Angela laughed. "She could of did better than that—"

"Excuse me," a dark-skinned brother interrupted, "I'm tryin' to get a drink."

They turned and looked at him; his accent caught them off guard. They stepped over to let him pass, checking out this rude man with what seemed to be an attitude. He stood about 5' 9, medium build, slight to the slim side, and had a close cut and a perfectly shaped beard. The gear he wore complemented his physique and the occasion. His beige linen pants that tied in the front and his silk brown shirt won him points for coordination.

As the bartender sat his drink on the counter, the stranger turned to reach in his pocket and caught Monica's eye. "I'm sorry—would you ladies like a drink? Tell her what you want."

"Alizé please," Monica said.

"And you?" He stared straight into Angela's eyes. She was very attractive to him. In his mind, he'd had her before. *Or a bitch just like her.*

She stared back. His long eyelashes and sleepy eyes made her weak, but the scar on his neck and the tattoo on his forearm made her see a man that was not for her. "The same," Angela told the bartender.

The stranger pulled a small stack of brand-new money out his pocket, pulled off a fifty, and gave it to the bartender. They couldn't help noticing the thick gold bracelet that matched the chain with the iced-out medallion around his neck. He picked up the drinks and handed them to the girls. That's when they caught a glimpse of the beautiful gold Rolex with the diamond face.

It sent chills through Angela's body. *He didn't look as good as Ray, but his style and persona made up for it in every way.* She instantly took him as thug, a hustler, and she made a promise to herself that she was never going to go that route.

"Thank you," the girls said smiling.

"No problem. It was my pleasure. What's your name?" He looked at Monica.

"I'm Monica, and that's Angela. Where you from?"

"Trinidad."

Actually he was from Jamaica, but he knew they wouldn't know the difference. And, really, it wasn't their business.

"My name is Damien." He reached out to shake their hands. "It was very nice meeting you both." He looked into Angela's eyes. "Hope I see you around." He touched her on her slim waist and moved her out of his path.

Angela didn't like him touching her, but he did it so smooth, she didn't say a word.

They went to sit down and check out the crowd when this tall dark-skin brother with braids stepped up to Monica. Within minutes she was on the floor throwing down.

Angela sipped her drink and stared at her friend, trying to figure out what Monica actually saw in these thug-type niggahs. Every niggah she talked to was straight hood, except for Quinn—he was a soft thug. He *played* thug, he dressed thuggish, but he was really soft.

As Angela's drink emptied, the waitress replaced it with another. "Who sent it over?"

When the waitress turned to point, the man was gone. She described what he had on, and Angela knew it was Damien. She scanned the club for him and saw nothing. Later, when she was on the floor dancing, she caught herself looking around to see if she saw him. *He wasn't all that,* she thought. *No better-lookin' than the other guys in the club, but his style* . . .

After the club, they were all standing outside. Rome had begun talking to this young lady. After his conversation got going, Angela and Monica headed to the car.

Monica got close to Rome and said loudly, "I know you not out here disrespectin' me . . . not in my face." Then she and Angela started laughing. So did the girl he was talking to and her friends.

"Girl, I'm hungry," the girl said to her friends.

"We gonna stop at IHOP on the way home," her friend responded.

"Which one you goin' to?" Rome asked.

"On Battlefield Boulevard," she said.

"Me too, shorty. I'll check you there." Rome walked off with Monica and Angela.

"If we ride way out there with you, boy, you gonna feed us," Angela said.

"For real. I'm hungry too. Goin' all the way out there behind some bitch—she ain't gonna give you none no way."

"Shit, she gonna give some to this *Lex.*"

"It ain't even yours," Monica reminded him.

"By the time she find out, it will be too late." Rome grabbed his dick. "I'll be done fucked."

They reached IHOP the same time as the girl Rome was talking to did. He said, "Peep that shit."

Angela agreed. "Damn, that shit is nice."

"Sittin' on all that chrome, windows tinted. Couldn't tell a bitch shit if I had that."

Angela got out the car. "That Land Cruiser is beautiful."

The girls Rome was talking to parked beside the truck.

"Come here, y'all. Get a table," Rome said to Angela and Monica. They walked inside and were waiting to be seated.

Angela pointed to the corner. "Look, that's that boy from the club."

"Damien."

Before they could even sit down, Rome came in and joined them. "Missed out," Monica said.

"Naw, I'm goin' over there after I drop y'all off—so hurry the hell up."

"You comin' way back out here?" Angela asked.

"Her crew live out here; she lives off Hampton Boulevard."

"Be careful, boy. Don't let that bitch get you in no shit," Monica warned. "I know she probably got mad niggahs."

"Why you say that?"

Angela told him, "Tellin' you to come over and she just met you. You ain't the first guy she allowed to do that."

"I know she ain't got no man," Monica added, "if she out here with her ass all out in that short-ass skirt. And her shirt's too small—bitch titties about to bust the goddamn buttons. Just don't be hard-headed, and be careful."

They had known Rome since Bayside Middle School and they had all hung out many nights before, from middle-school dances to Lake Edward house parties. And now they'd all be going to Hampton. They knew there'd be more good times to come. They also knew a lot of girls had a lot of shit with them. They didn't know her, but the way she was dressed—her weaved-in, long blond hair was put up in a french twist, and her nails were real long with airbrush designs—Monica and Angela knew the girl was fly. But fly girls can bring drama, and they didn't want Rome in no shit.

The girl walked over to Rome to tell him she would be home in about thirty minutes. She spoke to Monica and Angela and had a pleasant attitude. Even though they had negative thoughts about her, they could see why Rome was attracted to her. They noticed that her body was just as tight as theirs, but she had age on them. They also knew to keep her nails and hair up didn't come cheap. As the girl walked off, she took one last glance at Monica and Angela. She knew she had her shit straight, but she would give anything to have the natural beauty that Monica and Angela possessed.

As they got up to leave, Damien was at the counter paying for his meal. "Thanks for the other drink," Angela told him. "I didn't get a chance to say it in the club."

"No thanks is necessary, pretty girl," he said with

a partial smile and walked out the door. He didn't
even try to converse with her.

He's so short-spoken.

Angela watched as the other females tried to get
his attention, but he ignored them, climbed in his
truck, and backed out.

"That ain't no Land Cruiser, that's a LX450
Lexus." Rome looked at Monica and Angela. "Is
Hampton goin' to bless me with one of those?"

"We'll see, starting next week," Monica said.

Angela looked at Damien's truck as he pulled
off, and with thoughts going through her mind,
she started towards the car. She didn't know what
he did, but he didn't look as if he was worried. *But
why was he by himself . . . with that truck, jewelry, and
money? Why was he goin' home by himself?* She sat in silence until Rome pulled in front of their building
to drop them off.

"I'll get with y'all later," he said.

"Call us tomorrow," Angela said.

"I'm goin' to page you early," Monica said, "and
you better call me back."

It was Monday morning and Angela didn't feel
like going to orientation. She pushed herself to
the shower, threw on her sweatsuit, and ran out.
She arrived on campus and looked around for
Ogden Hall. She realized she was a long way from
high school. She started across the parking lot in
time to see Rome pulling up in his Honda Accord.
It wasn't the Lex, but it was his and it was depend-
able.

"What's up, girl? Ready for this shit?"

"Ready as I'm gonna get."

"Where is Monica?"

"She should be here. She stayed home last night."

"You stayed home with Ray last night?"

"He came over for a little while, but he didn't stay. He was still upset about Saturday night. He jumps to conclusions and wants to act all jealous and shit. Rome, you know I ain't doin' shit, and I haven't given him any reason to get attitudes with me. I love Ray, but that shit's gettin' old."

"Tell him. You have to let a niggah know when he's pushin' you away."

"Right."

They both heard a voice hollering their names. It was Monica coming across the lot. "What's up, family?" she said smiling. Then she punched Rome. "You was suppose to call yesterday."

"I chilled out with Quanita." He shook his head up and down like a kid with a secret.

"Who the hell is Quanita?" Monica asked as they strolled into the building.

"Girl from the club Saturday."

"That's the hoochie momma name?" Angela asked.

"The hoochie is real chill. I got over there Saturday night. She came to the door in a long T-shirt. We smoked a blunt, and all she wanted to do was talk. But I actually enjoyed her company, even though I wanted to hit. I picked her up yesterday in the Honda. We went and checked out a movie and got a bite to eat. Then we went back to her spot, and she broke a niggah off lovely."

"For real?" Monica asked.

"I'm going to keep seeing her. She's a junior at Old Dominion. She seems to be pretty focused, and plus, she got the bomb shit." Rome peeked around the room. "These bitches fine as hell—I'm goin' to have a ball over here."

The next week was full of campus tours and seminars. This was Labor Day weekend and after this weekend, it was straight business. Playtime was over. Monica and Angela decided to go to the Norfolk State game at ODU. It was always the shit.

The after-party was supposed to be at Pizzazz, but they decided to ride down the oceanfront. After strolling the strip for a while, things started to settle down and they were getting tired. "I'm ready to get a bath, kick back on the sofa, and chill," Angela said.

"Let's stop out Lake Edward and get us a dime sack first," Monica suggested. "You know we need that."

They started back up Atlantic Avenue towards 40th Street where they were parked. As they reached the corner of 32nd and Atlantic, they saw Damien and another guy walking up from Pacific Avenue. They stopped and waited for them to approach.

"Hello, ladies," Damien said, "this is my brother. He goes to Norfolk State."

Angela and Monica spoke, but never took their eyes off Damien. His brother, tall and lanky with dreads, no jewels, and a different color beaded necklace, was nothing like him.

"I keep running into you. It must be meant for us to spend some time together, or at least talk and get to know one another." Damien moved closer to Angela and looked into her eyes.

"Is that right?"

"Look, I'm having a small barbecue tomorrow. It's going to start about five. Page me, and I'll give you the directions, okay? Bring Monica along. You both should enjoy yourselves."

They agreed to call and headed home. "We goin' to his cookout?"

"I don't know. I'm still kind of unsure about him; I'm not tryin' to get mixed up in any shit."

"He just asked you to come to a cookout, not move the fuck in with him. He probably got a girl anyway."

"No bullshit."

Chapter Five

"I'll see you in a little while," Angela yelled as she walked out the door Sunday morning. It was early, but she was used to getting up for the early morning service instead of waiting until 11:30. She never cared for church too much and usually got upset with her mom for making her go, but ever since her mom and Ken joined The Faith Uphold Christian Center, she kind of looked forward to going.

As she sat in church, she listened to the pastor go from Scripture to reality, and reality to Scripture. The pastor's theme was, "You don't know what God has in store." She then realized that God would not allow her life to be turned around by sending a hustlin'-ass player to stand in her path. Maybe she would meet a successful businessman or doctor like Ken, someone who would push her, stand beside her, like she had always seen him do for her mother. *I'm not supposed to be thinking about men in church. My mind is supposed to be on what blessings*

God has in store for me, not what man is trying to inter-
rupt my life.

Angela opened her condo door. *What am I going*
to wear today? She tapped on Monica's door. "What
the deal, girl?" There was no answer, so she knocked
harder to override the sounds of the stereo coming from Monica's room. *She might have company.*
Usually she listens to rap, but she's playing Faith Evans.
    "Monica!"
    "Yo, I'll be out in a sec." Monica's voice was low
and sluggish, and Angela could barely make out
what she was saying.
    Angela walked away with a confused look on her
face, wondering who Monica was entertaining. "I'll
see you later," she said out loud. "I have to find
something to wear." She looked at her Levi jeans
shorts again. She knew she would be banging in
them, but she didn't want to come off as a young-
ass hoochie. Then it hit her, she had on a red thin
skirt that buttoned up the front, red heels, white
stockings, and blouse. She pulled her white top
out that came down just above her waist, so her flat
stomach would show. She then removed her slip
and stockings so that the thin material would slide
and flow with the movement of her perfectly shaped
ass. Then she undid several buttons from the bottom of the skirt so a little thigh would show. Then
she slid her foot into her red, open-toed sandals.
"Good God." She smiled, feeling proud of how she
put that together so well.
    Just then Monica came out of her room.
    "We still—" was all Angela could get out before

Monica covered her mouth. She didn't want Quinn to know about the cookout.

Angela whispered, "Sorry. So what up, girl?"

"Not a thing."

Quinn came out of Monica's room sparking half a blunt. "How are you, Angela?"

"Fine now—since you got the medicine. When you goin' back to Petersburg?"

"In a few. My man leavin' about two. I'm going to meet him at my moms. I'm outta here." He gave Monica the blunt, kissed her, and headed out the door.

"So what's up, girl?" Monica asked.

"I'm down, girl."

Angela went to her room to get Damien's number. When she called, a girl answered, "Hello," catching Angela off guard.

"Yes . . . can I speak to Damien?"

"Hold on."

Angela held the phone, wondering if she called at a bad time.

"Yeah." The voice with the accent came through the receiver.

"Damien?"

"Who is this?" Damien sounded stern.

"Angela."

"Heah, girl, how are you?"

"Fine. I called for directions."

Damien rattled off the directions. "Got it?"

"Yes. See you about five."

Angela and Monica arrived at Damien's house about 5:30, surprised at the beautiful home. There weren't many cars in the front: the two cars he'd mentioned, a Dodge Intrepid, a black Tahoe with Jersey tags, and a Cadillac STS sitting on chrome.

As they approached the front door a young lady welcomed them in. She was a little on the heavy side, about 5' 4, wide hips, and very large breasts, but the outfit she wore, she wore well. "Hello, come on in," she said.

"Thank you," Angela said. "We're looking for Damien."

"Sure, I'll get him. I'm Rhonda, Damien's sister."

"I'm Angela, and this is Monica. Nice to meet you."

"Everyone is in the back," Rhonda said, turning to walk away.

They began to follow her. When they got to the sliding glass door to go out back, it opened and Damien appeared, acting surprised to see them. "See you found it." He looked towards Angela. "There wasn't a problem, was it?"

"No, you gave good directions."

"Would you like something to drink?"

"Yes," Monica answered.

"Show her where everything is, Rhonda."

"I'm okay." Angela looked at her surroundings. "I like this."

"Let me show you around." Damien took her hand and headed to the front to give her the grand tour. They walked into the living room. The older-looking couch, coffee table, end tables, and the pictures with the gold frames hanging on the wall gave her the feeling that the room was for show, not entertaining. They strolled through to the formal living room and stepped out into the dining area, which gave her a clear view of the large off-white marble dining table with matching chairs and china cabinet. The table was set for eight people to sit and have a formal dinner. Damien stopped in the oval doorway and looked back at Angela admiring his shit. He stepped back so she could slide through and get full view of the eat-in kitchen and family room.

Angela soon realized that Damien's home was more extravagant than her parents'. *How could a young man not much older than me afford something like this?* She always heard of hustlers making money, but she'd never met anyone who had it like this.

She watched him as he guided her into his sunken family room with the marble gas fireplace. She tried not to stare at him, but he looked so good. She focused her attention back to the house. In his family room he had dark-green leather sectional with a beautiful glass table and the 52" Hitachi big-screen television.

"Come on, let me finish." He walked up the circular steps.

"How many bedrooms do you have?"

"Four, counting the bonus room over the garage." He entered the room over the garage. The audio system that covered half the wall was the first thing to catch her eye, then the nine-foot custom pool table that sat in the center of the room.

Damien focused his attention on Angela. *She is beautiful, but just like every girl, she's just out for the paper. No total commitment.* By her being so young, he knew she was about games and trying to explore her options. So he figured he was just going to show her a nice time, nothing more.

He held her hand and showed her the other two rooms. "This is it." He opened the door to his room. "Please excuse the mess, but this wasn't the plan. Or I would of straighten up." His accent was killing her.

She entered his room and her knees weakened. The king-size bed had a large column bedpost that made her think of royalty. Opposite the bed, was another gas fireplace next to the sitting room, which held a love seat, chair, and small circular table.

They walked into the bathroom.

"Damn. This is the size of my brother's room."

The jacuzzi tub was large enough for four people. In the corner was a separate stand-up shower, his-and-her sinks on the other wall, and a huge closet.

This niggah home is beautiful. How the fuck did he achieve this? "How old are you, Damien?" Angela's voice sounded soft and shy.

"I'm twenty-two. Why you ask?"

"I was curious. Do you live here alone?"

"No, my brother stays here too."

She found herself daydreaming about spending time with Damien. He had her attention, but she was going to fight this. She could never see herself spending time with a hustlin'-type niggah.

"So how old are you?"

"I'm eighteen."

He laughed. "How did you get in the club?"

It was the first time she saw him smile; he was usually real stern and serious.

She smiled. "Don't ask."

He looked at her beautiful smile. *Damn, eighteen.* Then it hit him. *Maybe I can mold her into the woman*

I want. He imagined her lying nude in the middle of his bed. It was picture-perfect. He didn't want to just fuck her, he wanted to make her fall in love with him, want him, desire him. Then he would have her mind and body.

He leaned back on the wall. "So what do you do?"

"I start classes at HU in a few days. I also work part-time at a lawyer's office."

"Where?"

"Off Freemason."

He smiled. "Robinson down there?"

"Yeah," she said surprised. Then she thought about a lot of young boys that went to see Robinson, local hustlers who had been caught in up in some bullshit. She could not hold it in any longer. "What do you do for a living? How do you afford this at twenty-two?"

"My father passed away when I was twelve, and when I turned twenty-one, I got my trust fund and came to Virginia. I bought this, and I opened a clothing store off Chesapeake Boulevard in Norfolk and it's doing quite well. Do that answer both your questions?"

"Yes," she said, giving him the benefit of the doubt. She still felt he dealt drugs. "So where is your girl, Damien?"

"No girl, Angela, just me."

She had a look like she didn't believe him.

"So where's your man?"

"I don't know. He's somewhere."

Instead of pursuing it, he figured he would leave it alone and just go for his. He leaned over in her ear and whispered, "I'm your man and I'm right here. Soon, you going to have to make a choice." He stood in front of her, put his hands on her waist, and kissed her on the cheek. He took her hand once again. "Come on, let's get back downstairs."

Once there, they walked to the back and stepped out onto the deck that expanded the length of the house. On both ends sat large grills filled with food. Everyone was eating and enjoying the music.

Monica was standing with Rhonda. "So who lives here, Rhonda?"

Angela waited for her to answer, to see if it matched her brother's.

"It's Damien's house, and my other brother came down to go to school. Almost everybody here leaving after the cookout; we got to get back to New York."

Monica reached out and tapped Rhonda as if they'd been friends for years. "Where is his girl? I know he got one."

"He haven't had a main girl for years. He just has friends."

Angela looked at Rhonda. "Are these all his friends?"

"No, just associates and people we know. I can say this—he had good things to say about you. I wish he could find a chill girl. Not no money-hungry-ass bitch. It's plenty of them out here, and all they get is played," Rhonda said as she walked away.

Damien came outside with a Backwoods in one hand and one behind his ear. Two girls came outside behind him. They sat down and began talking and smoking.

Angela looked on and actually felt herself getting jealous. She wanted his attention, the same way she had it earlier—undivided. She was almost ready to tell Monica she was ready to go . . . until Rhonda came back over with a drink and a blunt.

"Do you all smoke?"

"Hell yeah." Monica reached out.

"Who's the girls with Damien?"

"Those two girls over there are from New York. They came down for Labor Day. Pretty as hell, aren't they? Those are the two most rude bitches you ever seen. The one on the left standing up is China, and the one wearing the green top is Maria. We know them from 'Up Top.' They're mad cool; just don't get them wrong."

As Angela took the blunt and hit it, Damien looked dead into her eyes. She looked back like she had an attitude. She knew she had no right feeling like this, so she knew it was time to go. "We're going to get ready and leave."

"Already?" Rhonda asked.

"Yeah, come on, Monica." Angela headed for the sliding glass door.

By the time she went through the house and reached the front door, Damien came inside, the usual stern look on his face. "What the fuck! You just walk out without saying shit to me." He stood directly in front of her and stared into her eyes.

"Well, it seemed like—"

"I'm not talkin' to you."

Monica stood there. Didn't say another word. She could tell he wasn't playing.

"You were busy—that's why I didn't bother you."

"No, you don't just leave me without sayin' anything. That's rude . . . you understand what I'm sayin'?"

"Yes," she said like a hurt child.

"Come here; you're not leavin' now." He took

Angela's arm. "You can go back in there, Monica."
Then he and Angela walked out front. "These are
my friends, you are my friend—I have to mingle
with everyone. My peoples are leaving in a little
bit.

"This new movie started Friday, and I want to
see it tonight. It starts at 9:45. You can give Monica
your car to drive home when she's ready, but you
are mine for the evening. What did I tell you upstairs? Tell me my exact words."

"You're my man and you're right here, and
soon I'm going to have to make a choice."

"Okay. Now let's go back in."

The way he came at her scared her in a way, but
she liked the way he took charge—telling, not asking everything.

She went in the back and started talking to
Rhonda and Monica. Damien came back in and
walked over to them. He sparked the Backwoods
and began talking to Rhonda.

Monica and Angela just stared, not understanding a word.

He passed the blunt to Angela and walked back
over to China and Maria so he could finish talking
business.

The rest of the evening went pretty fast. Before
long everybody was leaving.

"Don't play with my brother, girl," Rhonda whispered in Angela's ear. "He's all I got." Then she
turned and left.

How could she tell me that? Angela thought to herself. *I'm not his woman; I'm Ray's woman.* Then she
gave Monica her keys to drive home.

"You need some gas, Angela. Remember, you
were going to get some on the way back home?"

"Let me get my purse."

Before she could turn, Damien reached in his pocket and handed Monica a twenty. "I'm going to change," he said. "I'll be ready in a few." Then he ran up the stairs to his room.

Monica asked her, "Are you going to be all right?"

"What you think?"

"Just be careful and go straight home. Call me when you get through the door."

Angela went back inside to wait on Damien. His brother had run to take his friend back to campus, and now they were finally alone.

She decided to give him a hand with cleaning up. She started to straighten up his kitchen, but when he came downstairs—he had his shirt in his hand—her body got a certain jolt that she'd never felt before. She'd never seen so many beautiful tattoos. She quickly studied his body and ran her eyes past the scars and across the tattoos. Her body began to moisten. She could also smell the sweet aroma of his Black Jeans Versace cologne.

They stumbled around each other until everything was fairly clean, then they were out the door. They got in the LX450, and he threw in Tupac's *Me Against the World.* They jammed all the way to the movies as the weed smoke filled the Lexus truck.

Throughout the movie Angela wondered if she was going to be faced with him asking for sex afterwards. She loved Ray and didn't want to cheat on him or hurt him, but she didn't know if she could tell Damien no, or even if she wanted to.

When the movie was over he walked to the truck and jumped in, tossing a D'Angelo CD. Before they reached the condo, he hit the track so that "My Lady" could come on. Damien reached out, took her hand as the song played, and kept hold of it until he reached her front door. "I enjoyed you today."

"I did too."

He leaned over and tapped his cheek for her to give him a kiss. She did and walked inside on a real high. *Compared to Damien, the weed didn't do shit.*

Chapter Six

The next morning Angela woke to Ray ringing her phone. "Where were you last night and yesterday evening?"

"I told you I was going to a cookout with Monica."

"No, you didn't, Angela."

"Well, I meant to. Look, I'll call you as soon as I get up." She hung up the phone before he had a chance to respond.

Thirty minutes later, hard knocks at the door woke up Angela.

"Get the door, Angela," Monica yelled from her room. Monica opened the door to Angela's door. "Angela, that boy out there banging on the door."

Angela wiped the sleep from her eyes. "Who?"

"Ray."

She opened the door. "What the hell is wrong with you, Ray?"

"No—what the hell is wrong with *you*. You been actin' funny lately, and I want to know what the deal is."

"Ray, you need to calm down and stop yellin'."

"Don't tell me what the fuck to do. Let me know what's up right now . . . because if this is how our relationship is goin' to be, we're goin' to have problems."

"Look, Ray, I love you and I don't know why you trippin'. Calm down."

He gave her a hug. "Baby, I love you too. But we haven't been spending a lot of time lately; I just have to learn to deal with it."

"I'm going to lay back down. Why don't we get together later . . . please . . ."

"Can I lay down with you?" He followed her to her room and climbed in bed beside her. He slid real close to her and put his arms around her. He held her and thought about how much he cared and all he would do to hold on to her. He began to caress her body and slid his hand up her thigh, then across her stomach and up to her breast.

She moved his hand. "Please, Ray—I'm tired."

He relaxed for a minute then decided he would try again.

She sat up with an attitude. "What don't you understand?"

"What's the fuckin' problem? If you stop smokin' so goddamn much, you wouldn't be so tired. Then maybe you'll feel like fuckin' me."

"Who are you talking to?" She raised her voice. "Maybe I'm not fuckin' with you because you are weak, a weak-ass punk—"

Before another word could come out her mouth, he slapped her, and she fell to the floor, crying hysterically as if he had really hurt her.

"Get out! Get out, or I'll call the fuckin' police!"

"I'm sorry . . . I-I didn't mean to. I really am."

"Fuck that! Ain't nobody goin' to be puttin' their hands on me. Get out!"

"Ray, it's best you leave right now. I don't want to call the police, but you got to be out your mind hittin' my girl."

"This between me and her Monica; stay out of it."

"Fuck that! You can carry your ass up out of here. Put your muthafuckin' hands on me and they'll carry you out this bitch. I'll fuck you up. But guess what—today they goin' to lock your ass up."

Monica took the phone and dialed *9* and *1*.

"Monica—"

"Bye, Ray. I don't want to hear nothin'. You know if I hit this other *1*, that no matter what I say, they're goin' to come out here, and I will tell them what happened." Monica hugged her friend.

Ray turned and left, and they stood there hugging each other.

Angela knew this shit was about to end and was really hurting inside. She still loved him, but that shit he just pulled was inexcusable. She still couldn't believe what just happened.

Ray rode down the street thinking about what had just happened. If he could rewind time, he would have waited for her to call him back and never went over there. Seeing that he had to face his actions head on, he wondered what could be done to rectify the situation.

He had been feeling fucked up all summer, and the fact that he was supposed to take over the family business was also bearing down on him. He wanted his own life; separate from everyone. Just him and Angela.

Since graduation his plans had changed from working in the family business to going in the military as an officer: Leave and go in the reserves now; return and be back to start school the following semester at Norfolk State University.

The following day he went to see a recruiter and got everything set to leave. The only hard thing was being separated from Angela. He wondered if she would even care. He tried calling her, but there was no answer. Feeling sick and desperate, he began talking to the answering machine. "I know *sorry* is just a word, Angela, but I am really sorry. I don't know what got into me, but I really have something to tell you. Please call me before Thursday. That's when I leave, and I need to talk to you before I go. Please call. I love you."

Angela woke up bright and early, excited about her first day of college. Everything was perfect—except for the left side of her face. It was still slightly bruised. *Thank God, he hit me with an open hand and not his fist.* Either way, she saw stars. She hardly ever wore makeup, but just a little was necessary.

As Angela entered Ogden Hall for her eight o'clock class she thought, *this isn't much different from my high school.* She wanted to see that seventy-five-to-eighty people-in-a-class shit she'd heard about.

Her instructors just spoke on what was needed and expected of them. By about noon she was done for the day.

Angela decided to go home and relax before going to work at 1:30. She walked inside the condo and hit the answering machine. Her father had called because he hadn't heard from her and then she heard Ray. His voice and message began to soothe her mind. She listened as she thought about him leaving. *Where the hell could he be going?* Then she heard a knock at the door.

It was Ray.

She let him come in to hear what he had to say.

He took the time to explain what had him so angry and why he ended up taking his frustrations out on her. Ray continued to inform Angela of his new plans.

She was surprised but let him know she was behind him. She walked in her room to change for work.

Standing in her doorway, he watched as she stripped down to panties and bra. He eased up behind her, put his arms around her and began kissing her passionately. He removed her bra and began to caress her breasts, then removed her panties and laid her on the bed. He stood up and removed his clothes in seconds and slipped on a condom.

As they kissed again he brought himself down on top of her and eased inside. She moaned and he began to move in and out at a fast pace. Looking down at her, he wondered how he could ever put his hands on her in a negative way. She was beautiful, and loving her was all he wanted.

She opened her eyes to meet his, and relaxed

her body—the picture of Damien came in her head. She began to imagine Damien making love to her and she began to move, moan, and then quickly opened her eyes to catch herself just in time, as she felt his body stiffen, and shake.

He stood up and removed his condom while walking into the bathroom. She finished getting dressed, and they walked out together.

She entered the office and figured someone had to be in love. In front of her were twelve beautiful red roses. "Mrs. Stevens, who received roses today?" Angela asked in a most professional voice.

"They came for you earlier."

"Really." *It had to be Ray wanting to show me he knew he was wrong and he was really sorry.* She hurried over and pulled out the card. It read:

> *I really enjoyed your company and would love to see you for dinner. Page me and let me know what time you get off.*
>
> As Always,
> Damien

She felt good; no one had ever sent her flowers. Damien sent her flowers for no reason at all; just to ask her to dinner. She sat down and got herself started on her work. After about an hour she paged Damien. Thirty minutes passed and he still hadn't called back. She paged him again, and he called back immediately.

"What's up? Look, just page me once; sometimes I'm tied up. If you do it right, then you know it went through, and I will hit you back, okay."

"All right. Thank you, they're so beautiful."

"Glad you like them. What time you get off?"

"Five thirty."

"So I'll see you then; I'll be in front at five thirty."

She kept looking at the flowers as the hours passed. *He is very sweet.*

The other night at the movies she was concerned with him wanting some ass afterwards and didn't allow herself to get into the movie. But she never even thought about him not even thinking of her like that. He surprised her, and it made her wonder why he didn't.

She tried to imagine what it would be like to make love to him. Would it be tender or rough? Fast like Ray, or will he take his time? She drifted deeper into a daze, picturing him licking her all over like she'd heard Monica and other girls talking about, but had never experienced. She thought about the conversation her and Ray had about oral sex. He'd said he would if he was married and not until. She'd vowed never, under any circumstances, to do it. The ring of the phone brought her back to reality.

"Hello. Robinson, Madison, Fulton and Williams. May I help you?"

"Hello, Angela. It's Ray"

She was surprised he'd called. "What's going on?"

"Wanted to see if you wanted to go out this evening. I could meet you at your house."

"It would have to be later; I have to finish up some work and probably won't get out of here until about eight."

"Well, give me a call when you get in."

Relieved, she said, "All right, I'll talk to you then." She was glad he called and didn't just show up trying to surprise her. She didn't want him to

go off on Damien and Damien end up getting
hurt.

She packed her things about 5:30 and headed
for the door. Angela opened the door, and saw
Damien sitting in the black truck on the rocky, un-
even street. She could see the smoke in the truck,
feel the bass vibration, and hear the new hot single
by Nas, "If I Ruled the World," pumping through
the twelve-inch "kickers" that sat in back of the
LX450. She walked over and climbed in, trying
not to show her excitement towards him, but she
knew her wide smile and jovial attitude would easily give her away.

She felt like a child whose parents had promised Chuck E. Cheese after school. Staring at her
with the remote to the radio in his hand, Damien
had his back against the driver side door. He smiled,
as he turned down the music and stared, amazed at
what he saw. "You are so fine, and your smile makes
me fuckin' weak," he said in a low, smooth tone.

She blushed as if what he said moved her, when
actually it was the island accent that weakened her.

"Do I rate a hug, a kiss or something?" He puck-
ered his lips.

She didn't know if he was playing or serious, but
since she wanted to kiss him anyway, she leaned
forward and kissed him.

"What you want to eat?"

"It's up to you, Damien."

"Shit, I don't know. We'll roll and spark this
ganja; maybe something will come to us."

"I'll spark; you start rollin'."

He pulled off thinking she must be the coolest,
baddest bitch he ever came across. She sat back,
enjoying the ride and company as he rolled down-

town through the expensive section of town called Gent. They drove up Colley Avenue into Park Place. She had heard a lot about Park Place and could tell the difference—as soon as he came out from the underpass, from the expensive Gent shops on 26th Street to the outside cafes on Colley Avenue, right into the drug-infested environment that surrounded the old run-down houses and abandoned buildings.

They drove for about twenty minutes until the blunt was gone. Finally they ended up on City Hall Drive. "So what you decide?"

"You driving and I'm with you; go anywhere." She looked over at Damien as she passed the blunt. *Nice truck, nice home, and he had money, and he always seem to be in a good mood. And he never hesitated to share his weed. That was much better than hearing a whole bunch of bullshit about how bad smoking was and how it fucked you up.*

Damien pulled in front of the Marriott, and the parking attendants took the truck as he walked inside to Stormy's Restaurant.

After they were seated, they ordered drinks. "So what's up, Angela?"

"Nothin', Damien. I told you I had a man."

"What about us? I like you. Never met anyone like you so young, but yet so smart."

"I know you have a girl, Damien."

"Look, lying isn't me. All I do is chill. If I'm not playing pool or out of town, I'm at home just chillin' by myself, and I'm tired of that. I want you there with me, to be mine. I need someone in my life to love me and someone I can put my trust into. I've chosen you, and you it will be."

"What about my man, Damien? I have to play fair."

"I can love you better than any man. We can be friends, but when you give yourself to me, it will be no game played from that point on. You'll be all mine. When you become mine, I won't have another man ever touchin' you again. It will be up to you."

When he asked the waiter for the check, she thought he was upset, or had an attitude and wasn't trying to show it. She was attracted to Damien and loved his style, but she loved her man. She couldn't take her eyes off him as they left the restaurant. *He was looking so good.* She felt good to be with him.

His style and persona made people look and admire. He acted as if he didn't care for the attention, but wearing the things he did and driving the Lexus truck, she knew he expected it. As his hand swung with each step he took, she noticed the shiny gold Rolex he had on at the club. She liked the way he shined. *It was different than being out with Ray, who could be boring sometimes.*

She stood beside him in front of the hotel, waiting for the attendants to bring the truck around. Just then, a group of businessmen came out of the hotel. Two stood beside Angela and stared her down as if she was by herself. "What is your name?" one of them asked.

Before she could answer, Damien put his arm around her and pulled her in front of him, ass to dick, body to body, and kissed the back of her neck. "You need to focus your attention elsewhere— *blodeclaat.* I'm not the one to disrespect."

Angela really couldn't understand what he said and figured the other gentlemen probably had a problem understanding too. But the tone and the statement—with no smile—was understanding enough.

He wrapped his arms around her waist until the truck arrived. "You like pool?"

"Yes, but I'm not good."

"Well, we're just playin' for fun."

They went over to Waterside, the inside mall that sat on the water, and which also included two clubs, a large poolroom, several stores, and numerous food courts. She had gotten into the game and was having fun. She'd forgotten all about Ray and the fact that she had to get up early until Damien asked what time her first class was the following day.

"Nine."

"Think it's time we go; I'm not tryin' to keep you out late until the weekend."

He drove her back to her car. Before opening the door, she paused and looked at him. *Should I just say bye, or is he going to ask?*

Damien told her, "Go ahead."

"Go ahead and what?"

"Kiss me. I know that's what you thinking— should I or shouldn't I? Angela, you can do whatever you want; I'm already yours. I'm just waitin' for you to come around. Please believe me."

"I do, Damien." She leaned over and gently kissed him on the lips.

"Let me know you got home safe."

"Okay, I'll page you."

"No, I'll be home. Just call."

She drove home floating on cloud nine, and no

sooner than she was in the house, she was on the phone dialing his number. After telling him how much she enjoyed herself, she hung up and called her father's house. She went to bed with Damien on the mind and her body aching for attention, but she forgot to call Ray.

Chapter Seven

With her busy schedule, the week went fast. Thursday was here, and it was the day for her and Monica to ride and drop Ray off in Richmond. She didn't want to see him leave, but he felt it was what he had to do.

Monica and Angela came straight back, not wanting to be on the road too late. When they arrived back at the condo, they continued the girl talk they'd started on the way back.

Angela hadn't talked to Damien since Tuesday and actually missed him. He had to go to the island to handle some business and wouldn't be back until the following week. Several guys had approached her, but she didn't have the desire to date any of them, even though some were quite nice. She decided to page him since he'd told her his pager could be reached anywhere.

A girl called back. "Hello, somebody page me?"

"No, I paged Damien. This is Angela."

"This is China—I met you at the cookout. He's out of town, but I'll try and get him your message if there is one."

"Just tell him if he finds time, I would like to hear from him."

"All right. Peace, girl."

Forty-five minutes later the phone rang. The caller ID read OUT OF AREA. She picked it up quickly. It was Damien. They talked for all of thirty minutes. He let her know he would be back in town next Thursday and that he looked forward to seeing her. She placed the phone down feeling something inside that went misunderstood. Inside, she knew that Ray was gone, and without her man being right there, she could put down her guard and let things flow.

After classes Friday she and Monica decided to go shopping. Her father's birthday was coming up, and she needed to find him a nice shirt or tie to take next weekend to Maryland. She stopped at Beecroft and Bulls, one of the men's shops known for selling quality men's clothes and accessories. As she was leaving out the door, someone pulled the door. Monica looked and kept walking, and Angela followed.

The cool, respectful sound of the man's voice made Angela and Monica turn to respond. His light-brown eyes glued to Angela. She caught him looking at her ass, and he quickly focused his eyes to hers.

Angela was stunned at the man's attractive physique, not to mention his clean-shaven face and flawless skin. "So, are you shopping for your man?" he asked.

"No, my father." She stared back into his eyes. *He's fine, and so well groomed.* He reminded her of Ken.

"Excuse me, my name is Mac, and you are?"

"Angela."

"How old are you, Angela?"

"I'm eighteen. How old are you, Mac?"

"I'm twenty-eight, and I want to get to know you, Angela. Can I?" He let the door go and stepped closer. "Tell me a little about Angela."

She smiled. "I'm a freshman at Hampton. I work every day, and I handle my own business."

"You're a very attractive woman." He reached in his pocket and pulled out his card to give to her.

She was impressed. Nobody had ever called her a woman.

"I would like to hear from you sometimes. I too have a busy schedule, but I'll make time for you. Have plans for tomorrow evening?"

Before she had a chance to think, she answered, "Not at all."

"Well, let me get your number, and I'll give you a call." He stepped over and opened the door to a S500 Mercedes Benz.

Angela stood admiring this fine gentleman in his Zanetti. The expensive Italian suit fit him like it was tailor-made. *That's probably a fifteen-hundred-dollar outfit.* When he handed her the pen, she noticed his beautiful Baume & Mercier watch and well-manicured hands. She asked him, "What type of work you do?"

"I own a real estate company: Lafarras Real Estate Group, in Hampton, by Buckroe Beach. I'm going to give you a call tomorrow, and we'll finish our conversation. It was very nice meeting you." He stuck his hand out.

Angela shook his hand and was all smiles. She walked over to her car, which Monica had pulled in front, and got in.

Monica was smiling ear to ear waiting to hear some shit. "What he talkin' about, girl?"

"He say we goin' to dinner tomorrow. We'll see if he call."

Monica laughed. "*Hope* he call—that niggah was fine, girl."

"He reminded me of Ken."

"I was going to say the same thing, because he look so professional, not like the thugs that we use to, with they pants hangin' off they stankin' ass."

"That's the type of man I need in my life, a professional man who will push me, hold me down, and help me out when I need connects."

"How old is he?"

"He's twenty-eight and got his own real estate company."

"That's the kind of niggah I need. Bet he don't smoke weed either, girl. He probably square and shit." Monica laughed. "Bitch got to do what a bitch got to do." They slapped hands, knowing that what she said wa'n' no joke.

* * *

Angela and Monica were awakened by hard thunderous knocks. Angela got up and opened the door, "What the hell, boy!" She turned to go back in her room.

"Had to take Moms to the store, so since I was up, best to keep goin'."

Angela yelled, "Monica," and climbed back into bed.

"Come on, Angela and Monica," he yelled from the living room so they both could hear him. "Get up! Let's bounce, baby. It's ten o'clock, and it's beautiful outside. Let's go to Military Circle and get some shit—fuck sleeping all day."

Angela yelled from her room, "Rome, you better carry your ass home."

"I know what the fuck to do." Rome turned on the stereo, but they didn't move. "Look, I had some extra money, and I was going to treat you to Piccadilly for lunch. And I might get y'all a shirt, or maybe even a skirt—as long as it's real short so I can see something." He laughed as they came out the room. "Oh, I got to say I'm going to buy shit before y'all 'ho's move."

Monica was standing in the doorway of her room wearing a thin, short nightie that barely covered her ass. "Hell, yeah! Why else would we get up on a Saturday morning?"

Angela was in the kitchen pouring something to drink. "So you buyin' gear?"

"Is spendin' money the only thing that move y'all?" Rome asked, rolling a blunt. "I'm buying shit like y'all got on—that's the shit I'm talking about. So let's all get in the shower together, so we

can hurry up and get out of here." He entered
Angela's room.

Angela headed back to her room. "Boy, you better get out of there."

"You better call Quanita," Monica suggested.

"She's been dismissed. Looking for newer and
better things. Look, if we not gettin' in the shower,
then y'all better hurry the fuck up."

"Give us a few," Monica said; "we'll be right
out."

Rome threw in R. Kelly's CD, *Twelve Play*, and
smoked his blunt until the girls were dressed and
ready to go.

They spent three hours in Military Circle, trying
to find the right gear. Now it was 4:00; time had
gotten away from them. They'd run into Fat Joe
and he'd promised to meet them at the condo
with weed and drinks about 5:00. When they got
back he was sitting in the car, rolling up.

"Boy, don't get in trouble," Monica warned.
"You don't know if these white folks being nosy or
what." They all went inside to catch up on what
was going on since they hadn't seen Joe in a couple weeks.

Fat Joe's moms had put in a word for him at the
hospital, so he was working there. She wasn't having him bullshitting around, now that he was out
of school.

Then Monica brought up the subject of
Quanita. "I enjoy her," Rome said, "but I'm lookin'
for something different."

"Why you change your mind about her?" Angela

asked. "You use to act as if you was all press to get with her."

"Too possessive. She tryin' to keep up with my every move, fussin' 'bout my time."

As the conversation continued, Angela and Monica let them know they were taking life as it came. Quinn was Monica's main thing, but she had her friends.

Angela let them know that she was trying to deal with being alone, and that she had some other dilemmas. Nothing she would discuss in front of Joe. The last thing she wanted was some shit to get back to Ray.

As they lit the last blunt from the quarter Fat Joe brought over, they all leaned back in deep thought, wondering where their young lives were headed.

Rome got a page from his brother and had to leave. Angela, Monica, and Joe were stretched out on the couches 'sleep, when the ring of the phone woke them.

Monica looked at the caller ID. "Lafarass Group." She had a confused look on her face. "Hello."

"Yes, may I speak to Angela?"

"Hold on, please." She handed the phone to Angela, who signaled that she would take it in her room.

Twenty minutes passed, and Monica heard Angela turn on the shower. She got up and walked in her room. "What's up, girl?"

"That was Mac," Angela yelled from the bathroom. "He's comin' from his office just across the bridge, and we headed out for a bit. Iron that top for me."

Monica came out and opened the sliding glass door and lit an incense to relieve the condo of the weed smell.

Angela was in her bathroom giving herself the finishing touches, when she heard the knock at the door.

Monica jumped up to get it and looked him up and down as he entered the house. "She'll be out in a minute; you can have a seat." She went into Angela's room. "Hurry up, girl—he waitin' on you."

"I am, girl." She sprayed on some Nine West, her knockout fragrance. Then she whispered, "What he got on?"

"Black dress shorts, beige shirt, and black sandals—he's definitely good to go."

Angela came out the room, and Mac stood up. "Good to see you again," he said, leaning over and kissing her cheek.

"Thank you." She headed for the door and sent Mac into a trance. He took a second to admire her class and body.

Angela had put on a little makeup to appear slightly older. She wore some khaki-colored silk shorts that moved with the sway of her ass and a matching top that she tucked in her pants. She set the outfit off with a gold scarf around her waist and gold sandals. She was the perfect vision, and when she walked past him, the smell from the Nine West perfume had him floating out the door behind her.

He walked down and opened the car door. *What a gentleman*, Angela thought.

He wore a gold ring full of diamonds on his left ring finger and an 18ct gold-and-steel Cartier watch. Which brought direct attention to his perfectly manicured nails.

He wasn't very talkative and she wasn't being out going, so they rode to Fisherman's Wharf with the relaxing sounds of Faith Evans playing. The conversation began to come alive as they sat waiting to be seated. "So what you studyin' at Hampton?"

"Mass communications. Where did you go to school?"

"I went to VCU and got my bachelor's in education, then went to Norfolk State for my master's."

"How'd you end up in real estate?"

"My father has a company in Connecticut. After I finished school, I was sending resumés out but had no luck. So I decided to try my hands at real estate until something came through, and here I am. It wasn't my plan, but it came off so well I couldn't ignore it.

"I sold real estate for three years, and then became a broker. My company is in its second year and we have revenues of over half a million, so it's coming along."

"You've done well."

"Yeah, but I'm not content in my business and I'm not happy in life." He spoke in a serious, low tone.

"Really? And why is life unhappy for you?"

"I want to make multi-millions with my business and I can't picture who I would like to share my success with. No one's in my life to share things with, to tell my day about, to just be by my side.

"I go out of town a lot—seminars and investment meetings with other real estate tycoons. Sometimes they're social dinners and formal parties. I'm tired of showing up alone. Yes, I have a busy schedule, but when I'm off, I really want someone there. Not just anybody, but somebody I could really get into. I asked God for it." Mac had a slight smile. "Maybe he sent you to me."

She smiled. "Maybe." *He's fine, successful, proper, and he shows respect.* The way he talked and the things he did made her feel special.

Dinner and conversation was going great. Mac suggested they do after dinner drinks at his house.

It was a short ride to Lafayette Shores, a very prestigious housing development in the middle of Norfolk where custom-built homes made up a gated community. *Goddamn this shit is phat,* Angela thought. *No niggah I know ain't got shit even close to this.*

They walked inside. As he strolled across the marble floor in the open foyer, she was temporarily blinded by the beautiful, but very bright chandelier that hung from the high cathedral-like ceiling. He guided her to his family room, where she noticed a smaller version of the same chandelier hanging over a deep-burgundy dining table that sat six easily.

He asked her to remove her shoes before stepping onto the plush winter-green carpet. She took a seat, and the soft bulky pillows smothered her body in comfort.

"Let me get us something to drink." Mac went over to a cooler with a glass door and pulled out a bottle of Moët and Alizé and held them both up.

"Alizé, please."

Mac picked up the remote control and aimed it for the stereo sitting in the custom-built cabinet centered inside the wall. The soft, easy sounds of jazz covered the room. It wasn't her preference, but she had learned to appreciate it by force when her mom and Ken played it. And if the right CD was on, it could be very soothing. As quickly as the thought popped in her head, David Sandborn came pouring out of the small Infiniti speakers.

Angela sipped her drink and allowed the smooth sounds to soothe her mind and body. Mac caught Angela as her eyes gently closed and she swayed her head slowly from side to side, allowing the music to take over. He eased down beside her and began to massage her shoulders and arms. Then he leaned closer and gently kissed her neck.

It felt good to Angela, so she just relaxed.

He leaned over and dimmed the lights, reached out with index finger, and touched her chin to turn her head to face him. What Angela thought would be a gentle kiss turned into a tongue swirling around in her mouth. Angela was stunned at his forwardness but did nothing. He pulled back and slowly pulled her into his arms. She leaned back, her back against his chest, legs up on the couch, enjoying the CD.

"Are you all right?"

"Yes, I'm fine. You have a gorgeous home. The African art is definitely a nice touch. Hope you don't mind me asking—but what do these homes run out here?"

"They range from two hundred fifty thousand to six hundred thousand. Mine ran me close to four hundred," he lied, knowing it was closer to three hundred thousand.

She continued to relax in his arms until the CD was through. "I think I better get ready and go; I have to get up early for church."

"Really. I attend Mt. Calvary with Courtney McBeth."

"Yes, I've visited y'all's church several times over on Popular Hall. Dr. Yeah. He's all right, but Faith Deliverance, Bishop Barbara Amos, is where I get all my strength," Angela said proudly.

"You should come visit again—like tomorrow." Mac spoke in a low voice.

She turned around to face him. "I would if you asked."

He stared into her eyes. "Would you?"

"Yes," she answered, staring deep into his.

He leaned over and kissed her gently, stood up, took her hands, and pulled her on her feet. Then he pulled her to him and gave her a firm hug. *Goddamn, this young girl feels good as hell in my arms.*

He dropped her off only to pick her up early the next morning. The service went well, and of course, as large as the congregation was, Angela saw many of her friends, and hoped it wouldn't get back to Ray. Actually she was enjoying Mac so much, her mind was free and she was enjoying life. They ended up spending the entire day, from dinner to bowling, to him having to stop at his office for some quick business. Mac didn't usually carry anyone while he handled his business, but he let her know that during the week his schedule was so hectic, it would be hard for him to get away and she might only receive phone calls. But today he had her and wasn't trying to get rid of her.

She enjoyed him and looked at him like no other guy she'd ever dated. He was a man with his shit together.

Chapter Eight

*D*amn! *I shoulda never laid down*, Angela thought as her alarm clock went off. She pressed the snooze button, but five minutes felt like one. She had to be at work soon and had no intentions of moving. Making it to class seemed like straight torture. She rolled over and stood up. "I got to get me some new shit." She looked through her closet. This weekend she was going to Maryland and would hit her father and Lenore up for some clothes.

She remembered a hair show that she'd seen in DC at the Four Seasons—Lenore had a big part in sponsoring it—where she got to see top-of-the-line fashions and hairstyles firsthand. She knew about two- and three-thousand-dollar gowns and hairdos that exceeded three, four hundred dollars. Whenever girls talked about clothes and hairstyles, she knew that they hadn't seen anything until they'd seen fifty drag queens strut their shit. Lenore told her, "If you really want to experience and learn some shit, keep your eyes on the queens."

Angela reached in and pulled out her pants suit and threw it on and was on her way out when Monica and Rome came in with upsetting looks on their faces.

"Why you lookin' like somebody died?" Angela joked.

"What's so funny, Angela?"

"Shut up, boy. What's goin' on?"

"You didn't hear about Dirt-Dirt?" Monica asked with a bewildered look. "He got killed last night."

"What happened?"

"Found him in the car shot in the neck. He was shot with a fuckin' shotgun. I told him to keep fuckin' with Bo. He know my brother the mutha-fuckin' man, but he said those Park Place niggahs was giving him better prices. My brother always said he would rather be safe and stick with niggahs he know, rather than try to get a deal and end up getting got."

"That shit is sad. All y'all need to stop sellin' that shit," Monica said. "That's the fifth person we grew up with out this way they found dead or has died a triflin' death."

"You right. Mo got shot on the basketball court out Lake Edward. And they found Duke and Rip robbed and cut the fuck up in Campus East."

"Then, they found Tee shot three times in the head by the dumpster, right beside the hole." Monica was referring to the dirty, man-made lake in Lake Edward.

"Everybody know that niggah, Mike-Mike, did that shit," Angela said. "And that shit wasn't even behind no drugs or money, though."

"Yeah! It was behind that triflin'-ass bitch, Pooh!" Monica said. "Now she fuckin' with Ski."

"Who haven't that bitch fucked?" Angela asked.

"Who haven't *Ski* fucked?" Rome said. They all forced a smile.

Angela had seen friends get killed, but she felt this one—Dirt-Dirt was all right with everybody. She wasn't sure where her life was headed, but she knew that she wanted to get the hell out of NW Virginia Beach. It had been hell going to Bayside, and it seemed to keep getting worse.

"We're going to his mom's house in a few," Rome said.

"I have to get to work, but sign my name on the card. Okay, Rome?" Angela knew better than to ask Monica.

Angela was at work thinking about the nice time she'd shared with Mac. All the guys she met always had that thug in them and showed it. Except for Ray. He was more laid-back and kind.

She decided to call her girlfriend in Maryland. She had been meaning to call, but now it was more convenient—and free. The call would be charged to the firm.

She had met Trinity the summer of '90, and they'd been friends ever since. One summer her parents came to their time-share at a Virginia Beach resort, and Trinity spent the entire time at Angela's house. They had always agreed that they would go to the same college and remain long-time friends. But Trinity decided she wanted to attend Howard University and tried her hardest to convince Angela to come to DC. Angela had her heart set on Hampton University, and neither could be persuaded to change their mind. Then Trinity got pregnant, and that settled everything for her. If she went to Howard she would have the help of family; in Hampton she would be on her own.

"Hello."

"Heah, girl, what's up?" Angela asked.

"Fuck you, bitch. I don't fuck with you."

"What, girl?" Angela laughed, knowing why Trinity had the attitude.

"You were supposed to call me last week. I bet your ass ain't even comin'."

"That's what you know 'ho'. I'll be there this weekend." They began yelling from excitement like old friends do.

"Really? Who comin' with you?"

"Probably Monica."

"Call me as soon as you get in, girl. They got a new underground go-go club. We have to check it out."

"Sounds good—I can fuck with it. You know they don't play that shit down here. All you gonna hear on 103 JAMZ is hip-hop and R&B. None of that go-go shit in the seven cities."

"I couldn't imagine not havin' go-go, girl. But, anyway, you know I got to get to class. I'm glad you caught me. Make sure you call me when you get in. Okay?" Trinity hung up.

As soon as Angela got off the phone with Trinity, it rang again. It was Damien. He was calling to let her know he would be back in town on

Thursday. He was in Tennessee at the time and was going to Charlotte Wednesday, before coming to Virginia. She soaked in every word. Angela was happy to hear from him. Not a day had past that she hadn't gone into a deep thought over Damien. Even the days she spent with Mac—he wasn't so powerful to push Damien out of her head. He couldn't get back soon enough. *What was his purpose for traveling all these places?* He was in Jamaica on vacation, *but what the hell was he doing in Tennessee?* Before she gave herself to him, they would have to sit and have a long talk.

Damien was trying to make his way back home to get close to Angela, without ever letting her know his business. How was she going to handle it when she found out that he was a hustler? He was far from the corner-, or around-the-way hustler; he was connected to some major players who reigned out of New York.

Damien met JB five years ago and his life took a totally different turn. He was young and working the corner, slinging hard from hand to hand, serving fiends making the local niggahs money. He had scraped and fought for his position. After getting in and doing his dirt, he was recognized by one of the higher-ranking moneymakers who used him as a mule for a while. But it taught him everything about trafficking drugs from state to state with little risk. As a mule and corner lookout, he was doing okay; living much better than the life he was used to.

One day while on the corner in Brooklyn, JB

pulled up in his S600 and motioned for Damien to take a ride. He had seen and heard about JB through people in the hood, but now he was face to face with this true hustler. JB, on the other hand, had heard and peeped some things about Damien. Word was, "the youngster had heart and determination to succeed in this street game."

JB began to take a little time with Damien, showing him how to bring drugs in the country from the islands and then move weight state to state, not block to block. JB really never had anyone to put trust into except for his sister, Jacqueline. But in time Damien came to be not only an associate, but a trusted friend. JB brought Damien into his clique, completing his trio. These three young men worked under JB, who had schooled each of them slowly and carefully.

In just a short time Damien was going to Jamaica, making moves back to the States, with plenty of work to distribute. Damien had befriended two girls, China and Maria, two ladies who he trained well and used as mules. He would travel to the island from different locations under one of his many aliases, while China and Maria would smuggle the work through customs and usually fly into Memphis, Tennessee. The drugs were then transported to North Carolina and distributed.

JB introduced Damien to several of his associates, the ones that he was to supply. They lived and worked out of Charlotte, Fayetteville, and the Raleigh/Durham area. JB told him, "Never do business where you rest." That's when he moved to Virginia to play it safe.

Damien's position was very important, and for this he received sixty thousand a month for his role in JB's organization, a small fee for the weight Damien moved in the Carolinas. Damien began running for JB two years ago, and he made his trip twice a month. He had become contented with his life and never had any intentions of changing for anyone, not even Angela—as fine as she was.

Angela hurried home after work to shower and change before Mac picked her up for the movies. She went inside and was stopped dead in her tracks when she saw two dozen white roses sitting on each end table.

Monica told her, "Look at our new decoration."

"Who sent you flowers?" Angela asked.

"Bitch, you the only one gettin' flowers these days—don't front."

Angela's response was all smiles. She picked up the card. It read:

> *ONE DOZEN IS FOR THE WOMAN IN YOU AND THE SECOND DOZEN IS FOR THE GOOD FEELING YOU GIVE ME.*
>
> > *YOURS TRULY,*
> > *MAC*

Angela's heart was deeply touched. This man, a real man, was so sensitive, and she felt she needed some sensitivity in her life. It would really make it complete.

Mac arrived at 7:00 just as he'd said, coming straight to Angela's from his office. (He was dressed for business.) Angela came out the room and, just as she had imagined, he was dressed to impress in his olive-colored Armani suit and shoes, Chanel shirt and tie, with glasses by Perry Ellis, prescription not fashion. She felt like he could take her anywhere and she would go without a fight.

"How are you?" she asked.

"Fine. And you?" He opened the door, allowing her to step out and lock it. He walked down the stairs and opened the passenger-side door.

Angela caught a glimpse of a different ring and gold Whitnauer. She liked the way Mac came across and wanted to be in his world.

They drove down Colley Avenue listening to Mary J's CD. Angela was all into Mary. Mac could tell by the way her body and head slowly moved to the smooth, laid-back sounds.

She snapped back when they pulled in front of the Naro. "What type of theater is this?" she asked.

"It's a regular theater, but they usually show documentaries that never make it to the other theaters. They're playing *Hoop Dreams*. I hear it's very inspirational."

After the movie they went to one of the many outside cafes that lined the streets of Colley Avenue. Then they took the scenic route to Mac's house, down Waterside drive along the water.

Once at Mac's home, he poured them some Grand Marnier. The sweet, smooth taste excited her and it wasn't long before she was feeling the effects of the sweet after-dinner drink.

Mac eased over, rested his hands on her shoulders, and removed her blazer. He leaned over and began massaging her shoulders as he kissed the back of her neck and allowed his hand to slowly slide across her breast. "Let's go to my room."

"I'm not quite ready for that, Mac."

"I want to be with you, Angela," he said with sincerity. "If I can't be with you, at least stay the night and allow me to hold you."

"Mac, it's not easy tellin' you no. I know if I lay down beside you I will give myself to you, and like I said, I'm not ready for that tonight."

"Okay, I'm a patient man, but as long as you know I want you to be mine—all mine—and I will make you happier than any man possibly could. Bet on it!"

"I believe you, and I promise when I'm ready I'll let you know. To be honest, I have unfinished business to deal with; it wouldn't be fair bringin' you into my shit."

"Handle it then; I'm not goin' anywhere."

"Thank you for being understanding."

On the way home all she could think of was Ray. She had to let him know that her heart wasn't in the same place. She didn't want to tell him while he was in boot camp, but the way he acted when he got upset before, this was the best way. It would give him time to deal with the situation before he came back home. She felt so funny inside, but this was something that had to be done. He had to know the truth.

"Will we talk tomorrow?" she asked as he pulled in front of her building.

"Of course, we will. Don't think otherwise." He

stared into her eyes. He knew she didn't know because she didn't fuck, but he wasn't pressed—his time was coming.

"I want to say thank you for the movie and dinner . . . not to mention the beautiful roses."

"You're beautiful, Angela, and very special. You definitely deserve to be treated like the woman you are." He got out the car and came around to open her door. She stepped out and into his arms. They embraced, and he kissed her gently on her cheek and stood back and watched as she walked up the stairs and into her condo.

Once inside she instantly pulled off her clothes and got comfortable. She rolled a blunt, sat down with a pen and pad, and began putting her thoughts on paper.

Dear Ray,

I hope you are doing well and this letter finds you in good spirits, even though you're in boot camp. I received your letter and almost cried at the way you said you were being treated. You've always been a strong-hearted person, so I know you will make it. I wanted to write you because I'm dealing with a tough situation. You've been the love of my life for a long time, but these days I'm feeling the need to get out and experience different things. I didn't want to send you a long drawn-out letter because I feel it would make things difficult. Everything seems to be going fine in my life. School is exciting and it's bringing new experiences. I want to be able to explore my options without hurting you. Things are changing and I don't want to go into detail, but I don't want you coming home to

*any surprises. Never feel that I don't care or that
you weren't special, because you could never be so
wrong. Please know that you will always hold a special place in my heart. You will always be a friend,
but you have to allow me to become a woman, learn
to be a woman, and the only way is through life experiences that I feel I'm ready for now. I hope you
can understand, because it means a lot to me that
you do. I wish you the best of luck in your training
and much success in life. Our paths will cross again
and I hope to see a greater man, much greater than
the one who left Bayside. I will always have love for
you and you will always have a friend in me.*

As Always,
Angie

Angela sat there with tears in her eyes. He was
her first real love, but she needed more excitement, the excitement of being introduced to new
things that Mac was capable of showing her. She
wanted a confident, take-charge-ass niggah like
Damien, someone who possessed the capability of
changing her life around. Mac was wonderful and
she enjoyed him. She could relax, but trying to be
a lady at all times was when the pressure began.
She didn't want to embarrass herself or him and
found herself watching her every action while trying to adjust to the new things in Mac's world.

Monica and Angela had the same schedule on
Thursday, so they rode together. Monica was drag-
ging, but Angela was hyped up. Damien was coming back today, and she hadn't been this excited

over anything or anybody in a long time. She thought, *How could I get so excited over a niggah that wasn't even my man?*

"Come on, Monica, I have to drop this letter in the mail."

"I don't believe you goin' to do it."

"I have to; I don't have a choice. He'll just to have to understand."

"He's going to come back home in a rage and fuck up you and your men." Monica laughed.

"I don't have a muthafuckin' man, bitch, and he ain't gonna do shit." Angela climbed in the car. "I'm going to see my dad this weekend. You goin'?"

"I'm not sure. I promised to help my grandmother with some things. If she sticks with her plans, then I'm out of circulation all weekend."

"Girl, I'm going to end up taking this trip by myself."

"You do know that Dirt-Dirt funeral tomorrow," Monica reminded her.

"You goin'?"

"Yeah. Rome and I supposed to be meeting at Fat Joe house at twelve, and all of us are going to ride together."

"I can't make it; funerals aren't me. I'm going to two funerals in this lifetime—my moms and my pops. I might go to my little brother's, but nobody else's, I'm sorry."

"When we stopped through the other day, his moms was so sad, she couldn't stop crying. I had never seen his brother before, but he was there losing it. Damn near brought tears to my eyes. I felt for them."

"Death is always hard to handle, but everybody gets through it with the help of God. I been in church all my life and I know with God's help you can deal with anything that comes your way. All you have to do is pray about it." Angela's tone was very serious.

"You right, but reachin' the point of dealin' with it is just hard. I know firsthand."

Angela reached out and took Monica's hand. She knew that besides Monica's grandmother and brother, she was the closest thing to her. Monica was like her sister, and she couldn't love her any more if they were blood.

Angela's schoolwork was starting to build up and she was either going to cut back on her hours at work or give up some of her extra activities. She had a test Friday and hadn't studied at all. She wanted to see Damien, but tonight it was going to be brief. She had to put first things, first.

She left work and went straight home. Damien had left a message to give him a call when she got in. She paged him and it was taking him a minute. She was getting ready to page him again but remembered what he'd said. She didn't want him getting upset. He finally called back to let her know he would be through about seven thirty and to be ready. He didn't want to miss the beginning of *Martin*. (*Martin, Living Single*, and *New York Undercover*—those were his shows.) She let him know she wasn't going to be out long.

He told her, "Bring your books . . . just in case."

She went in her room to shower and change. She slipped on her tights and a T-shirt and her old faithful Reebok Classics, since they weren't going out.

Chapter Nine

"There's Damien, Angela."

"How you know?"

"Don't you hear the bass comin' through the walls?" Monica laughed. "Give me some trees, Angela."

"I'm broke. Better call your man."

"Who? Quinn?"

"Naw, fat-ass Joe," she said laughing, going to the door. She opened it and Damien came in. He stepped to her and gave her a hug. She didn't want to seem too eager because then he would know she missed him, so she just held him for a second longer.

Damien felt it anyway. "Heah, baby, what the fuck is up?"

"Nothin' at all." Angel smiled.

"Heah, Monica, what the deal?"

"Nothin' much, Damien. How you? Got a blunt?"

"Monica," Angela said loudly.

"She all right. I had this for us to spark on the way to the crib, but I got more at the house."

He pulled out a fat-ass blunt and passed it to her. "Watch yourself—that shit straight killer." Damien noticed the flowers in the condo. "Somebody got mad love around here."

"You don't know," Monica said on the comeback, knowing Damien wanted to know who the flowers were for. "Now we need to find somebody to love my girl like that."

"I'm trying, baby. I'm trying. Let's go; I left my truck running." He headed out the door.

Angela looked at Monica and they just smiled. Then she looked at Damien as he walked around the truck, not even attempting to open her door. *He looks so thuggish at times, not like Mac.*

Rocking his navy blue-and-white Jordans that complemented the navy blue Nautica sweats, white Nautica T-shirt, and Nautica hat that came down so low over his forehead, you really couldn't see his eyes without him looking directly at you.

They climbed in the truck and started moving to the sounds of Lil' Kim banging in the truck. "Don't act like you scared to move the way you was throwing that ass around the floor the night I met you."

"No, I won't. I didn't even dance," she said with a slight smirk.

"I thought you didn't lie, Angela." She just smiled and pumped up the sounds.

As she moved to the music in a nonchalant manner, Damien kept glancing at her beautiful face and her body. *She is so fuckin' sexy.* Every time he'd seen her, she was looking like a doll. A doll that wasn't his. It was time he had tried to control his feelings, but she made it hard and tonight she was making it damn near impossible.

He turned the music down a little. "Why the fuck I couldn't keep you off my mind, girl? The whole time I was out, I thought of you. That's not good, Angela."

"Why not, Damien?" She stared into his eyes.

"Here I am thinking about you everyday and you're not even my girl. I've never been in a situation like that. How do I handle it?"

"I can't tell you how to handle your feelings. I'm too busy trying to deal with my own."

She started to tell him about the letter, but she figured, just like Mac, he was going to have to give her time to work things out in her heart and head. The things he was saying was what she needed to hear—that he cared and that she was on his mind as much as he was on hers.

They got to the house and she thought about him opening her door like Mac, but just as quick as the thought came, it disappeared. He was already at the front door. "Why the fuck you moving so slow. Are you sick or something?"

"No, I'm fine, but I ain't in no hurry."

"Damn, something smells good. What's that?"

"My brother made some jerk chicken with beans and rice." He uncovered the pots and pan in the kitchen. "Have some?"

"I've never had jerk chicken and I hate to waste your food."

"Bring your ass in here and taste it then."

She got up thinking that he was so rude, but she realized that he spoke quickly and didn't think first. That was just the way he came across. Even when he referred to girls as bitches. She noticed at

his cookout that he used it in his everyday vocabu-
lary while talking to Rhonda and other girls, and
wasn't out to offend anyone. That was just Damien,
he was a real niggah, like Rome and Fat Joe wanted
to be, like Rome brother Bo was, and what Mac
would never be.

He pulled a piece of chicken off the bone and
held it out for her. "Here," he said.

"I don't know where your nasty hands been."
She opened her mouth.

He placed it in her mouth and held out his fingers. "Do you like it?"

"Yes, it's real good."

He laughed. "Then lick my fingers."

"Fool, you crazy," she said, turning and walking
back into the family room and turning on the television.

"Turn that shit to *Martin*. Let's see what 'Marty
Mar' doin'." She started laughing.

"I'll get us a plate in a minute." He went over to
the drawer and pulled out an ounce of weed and
threw it on the table. He reached for the Backwoods
on top of the TV and sat down beside her.

She had never seen weed rolled in Backwoods.
She was used to blunts and White Owls. "Damn,
that shit strong."

"This that real shit—hundred fifty an *O*, girl."

He rolled three and lit one.

"Know what, you said on the phone that you
missed me and you haven't gave me a fuckin' hug,
kiss, or nothin'."

She leaned over and kissed him real slow. While
he was rolling the weed, he'd taken off his shirt off
and his tattoos were screaming at her to touch
them. "Did they hurt?"

"Hell yeah, but I'm a man." His accent came through hard, making him hard to understand. He passed her the weed and got up to put their plates in the microwave. Then he poured two glasses of fruit punch and put them on the table by her.

By the time they finished smoking, she was feeling real relaxed and was about to starve. They talked and enjoyed each show as they ate. She was in heaven, not trying to create conversation or watching herself. She was just being Angela and it felt wonderful, especially with someone that she cared about and enjoyed.

"You better pull your books out and handle your business. Don't be bullshitting when it comes to that schoolwork, your education. That shit is too important."

"I'm not." She went for her book, shocked that he even cared. He got up and poured them two drinks and lit another blunt.

"*New York Undercover* is my show. I gots to catch this shit every week. Take off your shoes and make yourself comfortable."

"I don't have any socks," she said.

"Hold on." He ran up the stairs and came back down with a bag. He'd brought her a T-shirt from Jamaica and some slippers that fit perfect.

"Thank you, Damien. That was sweet of you. I'm going to have to do something sweet for you."

"I could really use a massage. Can you handle that?"

"I think so." She leaned over and massaged his shoulders and back. Her touch was fucking him up. Her hands were so soft and warm, every time she squeezed it made his body weaker.

He turned to her and pulled her close as she put her arms around him. He kissed her real slow and passionate. Kissing wasn't his thing, but she was so beautiful. And letting their tongues touch was very stimulating. He kissed her neck and at the same time massaged her back. He was feeling high as shit, so he knew she was on the same level.

As he kissed and caressed her, he felt that this was their time and made his move. He slowly moved his hand towards her breasts. He heard her sigh as he laid her back on the couch, rubbed her back, and undid her bra. Slowly he pulled up her T-shirt and kissed her stomach. She sighed again softly from the kisses that were now arousing her.

I said this wasn't going to happen, Angela thought to herself, but her body loved the attention and her mouth couldn't open to say stop.

As his tongue eased up the hairline on her stomach to her beautiful breasts, he slipped one of her hardened nipples into his mouth and began to suck gently. He flicked his tongue across the nipple, sending a sensation straight to her inner thigh, where his hand was already resting. His touch kept going higher until his hand rubbed her vagina. She squirmed at his slightest touch.

He continued and she relaxed and laid her head back, letting out a sound that let him know to continue.

"Let's go upstairs," he said, taking her by her waist and leading her to his room. He hit his switch and the light from the gas fireplace lit up the room. One hit of the other switch brought the sweet, slow, sounds of "After 7." He guided her to the bed, slowly undressed her, and pulled back his comforter for her to relax on the burgundy Ralph Lauren silk sheets.

As he stood there undressing, he stared at Angela's beautiful brown body lying on his bed. He knew he had been with mad bitches that were fine as Angela and bodies even better, but she had moved him.

He moved closer and slowly ran his hand up and down her body as if to explore it carefully looking for faults, but there was none. He leaned down and kissed her lips lightly, then each cheek. Without lifting his lips, he let his lips move slowly from her cheek, down her neck and as he kissed and gently sucked. Damien ran his tongue into the crevice of her neck, slowly positioning himself to get a full view of her breast. He lowered his head and began kissing her breast. Then in a slow motion he sucked the nipple into his mouth and began to suck firmly; his tongue flickering at a rapid pace.

Her body began to move, and he could feel the rate of her heart pick up just as her breathing became heavier. He knew she was ready for him, but he had already vowed that he was going to be the best she ever had. He moved to the other breast, gave it the same attention and reached down and caressed her vagina. This wasn't to arouse her like he played it, but to test her. He ran his fingers across her vagina and then palmed her breast so that he could smell the finger he ran across her pussy. It was fresh. *Guess her momma taught her well.* And since she did, Damien left a wet trail with his tongue from her breast down to her vagina.

Angela's mind elevated into the clouds as

Damien's tongue worked his way past the lips of her pussy and into its wet waiting softness. As his tongue explored her insides, he moved so he could run his tongue from her clit to her ass in a continuous motion. She panted and began to get louder; her body was feeling what she never felt before. He reached up and took her hands, locking his hands and hers. He licked and sucked her clit until all her mouth could say was, "Please, please, please," as a feeling began to come over her body that left her shaking and gasping for air.

He came up and kissed her as her arms wrapped around him. He knew he should have gotten a condom, but he wanted to feel her—she was his and that wasn't going to change. He positioned himself to enter her, and she knew it was time to tell him she wasn't on anything and he needed to use a condom. But she wanted it to be perfect and didn't want to spoil the moment. When he entered her, she closed her eyes and let out a moan of pleasure. He stared down at her and slowly stroked her to heaven. He realized that she hadn't been really schooled—she barely moved, and her body was real tight. But she felt so good, her inexperience didn't mean a thing. As her breaths got louder, he got more excited and thrust even harder. She strained to open her eyes to see him staring down at her.

"Are you okay?"

"Yes," she said between breaths.

"You feel so good, Angela. God, you feel good." As his body started to tense, he felt the greatest feeling in the world starting to take over his body. "Are you on anything?"

"No," she said under her breaths. Her head

came up wondering what he was going to do. She felt his body speed up and then began to tense up. Then all of a sudden, he snatched out his dick, laid it on her wet pussy with the head sticking up, laid his body against hers, and enjoyed the feeling of nut squirting between their stomachs. They laid there in each other's arms and cum.

"I'm sorry," Damien said, "I didn't know what else to do with it."

"Don't be sorry. Thank you for being concerned and responsible when I wasn't." She squeezed him harder.

She realized as she lay there that nobody had ever made her feel that good. He was wonderful. She wasn't going to let him go anywhere. She just hoped she made him feel as good.

He got up and got a towel to wipe them off, and she laid there as he ran the water in the Jacuzzi, with bubbles. He walked over to the bed and picked her up, sat her down inside the tub, then walked downstairs. She sat relaxing until she heard him change the CD and Maxwell came on. He came back in the bathroom and got in and let Maxwell massage her mind and body as he bathed her entire body. She thought she was in heaven; she felt she was in love. She followed his lead and started to bathe him. He laid back and let her do her thing.

It was then she realized that she was entering into a zone she had never been in. She had never been the aggressor. Ray was always fast. Kiss, kiss, and—boom!—the act was over. But Damien had taken his time and made her feel shit she hadn't felt before, so she wanted to return the pleasure.

She reached for his penis and felt his manhood

harden again. "Stand up," she said. She began to rinse him off as she stared at the dick that also seemed to be staring at her. She said she would never do this to no man. *Why did this dick rate special attention? Because he made me feel so good.* She eased her mouth around his stiffening dick and began to suck with inexperienced lips, and lick with an inexperienced tongue, and each time her teeth hit it Damien jumped.

She wasn't the best and, from what Damien had experienced, far from it. But this was different. This was Angela, and he was going to accept it.

He was in heaven, and never will she ever regret it. He eased her to her feet and kissed her. Slowly he twisted her body so that her ass was up and out, which gave him easy access to slide in from the back. Her breath was taken as he entered her. She let out a sigh of pleasure. He was definitely the best she had ever had. They relaxed in the tub and held each other thinking about what had just occurred.

She cuddled up under him like he might leave. He didn't mind because he held her like she might sneak off into the night.

The next morning came quickly. Damien woke up, dick hard. He placed his dick under her butt between her legs and nudged at her. A smile came across his face as her leg lifted and invited him into the warm box that felt like no other bitch he had ever fucked.

"Damien, I have class at eight, and I still have to change."

"Okay, just five more minutes," he said without moving or opening his eyes. She sat on the edge of the bed and rubbed his back while he got in his five more minutes.

"Damien, it's that time. I also need to stop and get some breakfast," she said in a whining tone. He sat up. "Look in that top drawer," he said pointing, "and get that key with the remote on it."

She pulled it out.

"Take the truck, and I'll see you later."

"I get out of class at twelve and I don't get off work 'til five."

"I'm not going anywhere; I'll see you later. Look in the armrest and get twenty for breakfast and lunch. I got dinner. You are staying with me tonight, right?"

"Yes, baby," she said smiling from ear to ear.

When Angela arrived at the condo, Monica was getting dressed for class. Angela made a quick change, only to throw on some tights and the T-shirt Damien had brought.

"Why you rushin', girl? You got time," Monica said.

"I got to stop and get something to eat."

"Can I ride with you?"

"Sure. Come on; I'm out."

They walked down to the truck.

Monica grabbed her heart like she was having a heart attack. "Oh shit! Oh, hell naw. No, you don't got his truck, bitch. You fucked him, Angela? I know you did, but I got to hear you say it."

"No, I didn't fuck him. He fucked me, girl, and he fucked me like no other niggah have. You know most of these young niggahs like to just throw it in and you don't even be wet. This niggah ate my pussy until I was drippin', then he slid in and tamed the kitty cat." Angela laughed.

On the way to school Angela gave Monica the entire rundown of the evening, then finished up on the way home after class. Monica knew this guy had her girlfriend open, but since Angela had the Lexus truck, she figured that niggah had to be open too.

Angela's day was great, except for the time spent in class when it felt as if time was standing still. She was at work when she got a call from Mac. He had gotten off early and wanted to see her. She told him she had made plans already with her mother and the only way was to come by her office.

He couldn't get by the office that evening, so he made plans to see her on the weekend when his schedule was free. She wanted to see him because he had made such an impression, but right now, she was high on Damien—that's who had her head—and when she got off, he would have her body to go with it.

Chapter Ten

She left the office headed straight to Damien's house. She noticed a white Land Cruiser with Connecticut plates parked in the driveway. She knocked.

"What you knockin' for?" he asked.

"I didn't want to interrupt."

"I heard that." He gave her a slight hug and a peck on the cheek. "I'm tryin' to finish up some business, so I want you to come in and speak, but then excuse yourself to my room for a second."

She went into the kitchen and saw the two girls she'd met before, China and Maria. "Hello, how are you all doing?" she asked.

"Fine and you?" China responded.

"I see you found him," Maria added, throwing a pleasant smile.

"Yeah, he found his way back." Angela slid her hand across his stomach. "Y'all take care and maybe I'll see you later." She walked away going upstairs. *Damn, I like their style.* The diamond tennis bracelet, the rings, the long, beautiful manicured nails, the same style clothes that she'd seen in Lenore's closet, sexy, but yet conservative. She wondered if that was what Damien liked. Or did he want her to stay the same?

She heard the voice from the doorway. "What you thinkin' about?"

She turned to see Damien standing looking good as hell—new butter Timbs, dark denim jeans, and his orange RP55 T-shirt. *He must shop by the day. He always got on new shit, and whatever he wears, he wears well.*

"Oh! I was supposed to be going to DC this weekend to see my father, but Monica had something to do and I didn't want to go by myself . . . so I don't know."

"It will work out. Don't let the small things bother you. You look good today." He eased up to her and put his arms around her.

"Thank you. You not doing bad yourself." She held the medallion that swung at the end of his Cuban lynx.

"Thanks. Picked it up at the Coliseum Up Top."

"What's the Coliseum?"

"Mall in Queens with the entire first floor nothin' but gold. They be battlin' for prices."

"Sounds like the Jewelry Center in DC."

"Really, I have to check that out one day. You like jewelry?"

"Of course, but as you see it's not in the budget."

The doorbell rang. Then he heard Maria yell, "UPS truck outside."

He ran downstairs. About five minutes later, he was calling for Angela, as he said his good-byes to China and Maria, who were about to leave.

"Hold on, let me give this package to my brother," he said running up the stairs to his brother's room. He returned in minutes with smiles and a hype-ass attitude.

"What's up, girl? What we going to do?"

"It's on you, Damien. I know I have to change these clothes before we do anything."

"Want to throw on some shit to show your ass, huh?"

"Why you say that?" she asked with an attitude. "Can I ask you something?"

He smiled. "You can ask me anything, girl."

"China and Maria, their jewelry, them clothes, their nails and being fixed up all the time. Do you like that in your girl?"

"Nails done all the time—yes, I like that. Hair looking good—I demand it. Jewels—I really like on a woman, and as long as the clothes fit the occasion, I'm with it."

"What you mean 'fit the occasion'?"

"If you goin' to school or to a game, dress like that. Conservative. If you going to work, look like you look now, like you ready to handle some business. If you going to the club or if we going to a party, I want you to be the sexiest bitch up in that muthafucka—no doubt. I'll treat you like my little baby doll and dress you in real cute shit I like because I don't buy shit I don't like anyway."

"Is that right?"

"Damn right. You'll see." He headed out the door.

They arrived at her condo. "I have a TV in my room. I have to shower and change."

Damien sat on the bed and pulled out the Backwoods pack and began rolling.

Angela shut the door and put in a CD.

He continued rolling as she undressed to her bra and panties. He sat there as she walked into the bathroom, leaving the door slightly cracked. As the good weed started to sink in, he stared through the open door and thought about her sexy-ass body, how she tasted last night, how he made love to her and it was all that to him. He laid back and allowed his thoughts to interact with what he'd just seen. Along with the hydro, his mind and body was taken to a new plateau.

The opening of the bathroom door interrupted his thoughts. He sat up realizing that he had got turned on. His dick was hard as a brick. He watched her as she walked across the room to get some lotion.

"Will you lotion me down?"

"No question." He passed her the blunt and took the lotion. Then he removed the towel, and she laid across the bed. He applied the lotion slowly, then turned her over and finished up as he stared into her eyes, which began to get low from his gentle touch and, not to mention, the 'dro.

"You know I want you now," he said taking off his shirt.

She laid there as he kicked off his untied Timbs and let his jeans fall. She was so turned on by his dark skin and the glistening gold that rested on his neck and wrist. He leaned over and kissed her, and she jumped from the cold medallion touching her naked body. He reached down and let his Tommy Hilfiger boxers fall; she lifted her legs to accept him. And they fell into moments of intense sex.

Angela and Damien had just come out the shower and were getting dressed when they heard Monica come in. "Sounds like your girl got company," he said.

"Sound like Rome and Fat Joe. Them niggahs ain't company; they from school. We all grew up together," she said in a nonchalant manner.

"Do they know your man?"

"No, but they gettin' ready to meet him."

He smiled, leaned over, and kissed her. *Goddamn, this bitch gettin' to me,* he thought. Never had he been with a girl that made him soft inside. "So are you going to DC?" he asked.

"Actually, it's Maryland, right outside of DC. Why," she joked, "you goin' with me?"

"Sure, I haven't been to DC in a minute."

"For real? Only one thing, I was going to stay with my dad."

"Tell you what—we'll go, I'll get a room, drop you at your dad's, and pick you up later on Sunday."

"What you goin' to do?"

"Feel like drivin'? We can leave now."

"Let me get some clothes together then we can go by your house."

"Baby girl," he said taking her hand and looking into her eyes, "let's go now while I'm in the mood. I will buy you whatever you need, from your under-clothes to your shoes—I got you. Let me finish rollin' these 'Backs, and we out."

They walked into the livingroom where Monica and her company sat. "What's up, girl?" Monica pulled on a blunt.

"Not a thing. Heah, Rome, Big Jooooe," Angela said in a deep voice, punching Joe.

"What up?" Damien said, speaking to Rome and Fat Joe. "D." He gave the two guys a pound.

"We gettin' ready to go to DC," Angela said.

"Now, where's your fuckin' bags?" Monica asked.

"D said I'm straight," Angela said. She figured Damien didn't want niggahs to know his real name like that. Monica smiled at Angela, and Angela smiled back. They both knew Angela had found her somebody special, a real niggah.

Chapter Eleven

They arrived in the metropolitan area around midnight. The sound of Damien talking on his cellular woke her up. She tried to understand what he was saying, but couldn't. Noticing she was awake, he held the phone down and turned his attention to her. "You going to your dad house tonight, or in the morning?"

"In the morning. I want to stay with you," she said in a soft, sweet voice that made him soft inside.

He began talking on the phone again. He talked fast and his accent was hard, making it difficult for her to understand what he was saying. Moments later they were pulling in front of a home slightly larger than Damien's and just as beautiful. She knew they weren't too far from Baltimore, because she timed herself.

"This is my cousin. Not blood, but his mother and mine came from the islands to New York together when they were young. We lived in a little spot in Harlem about eight deep in a two-bedroom hole. He moved to Jersey when we were about fifteen. Everything I did, he did, and we looked out for each other. When I came to Virginia, he came too, but he said Norfolk was a little too slow, he had to be where he could have access to the city.

"You two the same age?"

"I'll be twenty-three in December, and he'll be twenty-two in November." They walked up to the two-level, contemporary-style home.

"*Blodeclaat!*" his cousin yelled as they hugged each other like only peoples could do without looking gay.

"Nothin', man, nothin'," Damien said.

"Who's this beautiful woman?" his cousin asked.

"This is Angela. Angela, this is my cousin, Noriega."

"Nice to meet you." Angela stuck out her hand.

"No, girl," he said with the same accent as Damien. Then he hugged her as if she was family.

Goddamn, this niggah's fine. Finer than Damien and Mac, but a bit too skinny.

Noriega was a slim, dark-skinned man. His hair was like silk, and pitch-black. Noriega's father was Dominican and lived in Miami. He made his money the same way as Damien, but through a different connect. His father dealt strictly with heroin and would get it to Noriega by different means, and Noriega would distribute it to his peoples in Baltimore, DC, Phili, and back in Jersey.

Damien and Noriega never dealt with anyone in New York anymore. They said once they got out, they weren't going back. They still went to visit their peoples, but it was only for a second. Even though Noriega had much more paper than Damien, you could never tell. He wasn't materialistic. He wanted nice shit and had nice shit, but never extended himself to look as rich as he really was. Nevertheless, he always respected Damien's hustling skills from the street to the penthouse, and Damien had the same admiration and respect for his cousin.

"Come on in and have a seat," Damien said to Angela as he walked to the kitchen.

"Ya hungry or ya tired?" Noreiga asked. "You can't be both—not in this bitch. 'Cause it ain't shit in here to eat. So if you're hungry, we got to go out."

"Starvin' cousin," Damien said with Angela seconding the motion.

"Salone," Noriega yelled from the bottom of the stairs, then back into the den. "As soon as she gets dressed, we out of here. It's Friday too." Noreiga's lady, Salone, walked in wearing a long, emerald-green, silk robe, with matching slippers.

Damien thought she was a goddess; Angela thought she was a model. She was tall, slim, very petite frame, but beautiful.

"This is Salone," Noriega said. "And this is my cousin Damien from Va. and his girl Angela."

"Hello," Damien and Angela said simultaneously.

"How are you? It's a pleasure to meet you both." Salone spoke with an accent that made Damien weak in the knees.

Damn! This bitch is beautiful. Where the fuck she from? Damien thought.

"Get dressed. We're going to find something to eat. And show Angela where they're going to be sleeping at tonight."

Angela and Salone walked away.

"And bring my boots I had on down." Noriega looked to make sure the girls were gone.

"Goddamn, D, that bitch phat as hell, and fine. With class too. Respect, respect."

"Naw, cousin, you always did fuck the baddest bitches comin' up, but you outdid yourself." Damien shook his head.

"I do all right." Noriega smiled, ready to tell his cousin his girl's credentials. "She from France. D, I hooked up with a French bitch, man. Got a degree from Howard in political science and works as a translator. I sent her ass back to school for her masters, but I'm gonna marry her ass before she graduates. Bitch not gonna get my paper and fly away. I'll have to move again. Bitch will make my body count begin to rise in the South." They both began laughing.

By now they were talking with such a hard accent that if the girls came up they would really have to listen to get the words.

"I'll drive." Noriega handed Damien the Backwoods to spark. He opened the door.

Angela eyes widened at the thought of how well Noriega lived. *Family with money,* she thought.

Damien gazed at the new E300. "When you get this?"

"That's her shit. Can't ride in that, because we can't smoke in that." Noriega opened the door to the new black four-door Tahoe. The boys jumped in the front, letting the ladies know they had things to discuss. They turned the music up just enough to enjoy the Backwoods and good conversation without being heard.

"She got any friends?" Noriega asked in his hard Jamaican accent.

"Roommate." Damien smiled. "Picture Salone

at eighteen with a body like Angela." They gave each other a pound.

"I'm comin' down soon. Salone friends are all studious and shit. Bitches got degrees out the ass, makin' good money, got they own shit, and ain't been fucked in months. Next time you come in town, bring some fly shit; I'll turn you on to these 'ho's. Invest your money in them—it will always come back to ya."

"All right," was all Damien could say with a spaced look on his face.

"Yo, man, I know you not lettin' that shit from Richmond fuck with you still. Don't do that shit, cousin," Noriega said, getting real serious.

"Go to Big Bob's," Salone said over the music.

"You want Big Bob's or some shit in the street?"

"Just grab some shit in the street. Where we hangin'?"

Nore decided to check out some of the Jamaican clubs that he knew about. He didn't hang out much, but with his cousin Damien by his side, he knew the night was going to be all right.

After a long night of partying, Damien and Angela were awakened by the smooth sounds of Maxell coming through the walls. They strolled downstairs to catch Noriega and Salone embraced, dancing around as if they were in another world.

"Turn down that damn music. Where the hell you think you at?" Damien said with Angela by his side smiling.

Noriega and Salone jumped as if they forgot

they had company. Damien and Angela began laughing hard because they had scared the couple.

"You two are crazy," Salone said.

"Make a niggah grab his shit—you know I'm fuckin' paranoid."

"We have to go to the mall." Damien picked up the ashtray with the half-smoked Backwoods and lit it."

"Hold on, we're going also. Then we can stop at Big Bob's to eat and I can find something to wear to the game," Salone said. "You know Howard and Hampton play today, don't you?" she asked as they headed for the stairway to change.

"What you goin' to do?" Damien asked.

"I have to meet Lenor at one at her shop." She stood waiting for his response.

"Then I'll drop you off and then get with you tomorrow."

A look came over her face that let him know he'd said the wrong thing. Maybe not the wrong thing, but it wasn't what she wanted to hear.

"Angela, what do you want me to do?"

"I want to go to the game if you goin'," she whined.

"How in the hell are we gonna do that?"

"Go to the mall, come back and change. Then I'll go to the shop with Lenor and either she can drop me back off or you come back and get me about five." She said it like it was nothing.

Who in the fuck feels like doin' all that? "All right then, that's what we'll do." He looked at her and promised himself that that beautiful smile would remain there forever.

* * *

When they returned from the mall and breakfast, they showered and all met on the back deck
by the pool. "I'm gettin' ready to drop her off at
her people's salon. I'll be back."

"Where's the shop?" Salone asked.

Angela told her, "Up near Georgetown, off M
Avenue."

"I'll drive you," Salone volunteered; "then I can
do some shopping."

They walked the girls outside to the car. Damien
reached in his pocket and handed Angela some
money. He put his arm around her neck and
pulled her close as they walked. "You can do some
shopping too. See you later." Then he kissed her,
and they were gone.

Noriega and Damien had run out shopping.
Damien wanted to pick up a gift for Angela before
she returned. When the girls did return, they never
knew the boys had run out because they were sitting in the same spots on the deck, sparking Backs
and sipping Henny XO.

The girls were gone a little longer than expected. When Noriega heard the door, he yelled
from outside, "Where the fuck y'all been?"

Salone screamed, "We'll be ready in a few minutes," and went up the stairs.

Moments later they returned ready to go. Angela
asked, "What you waitin' on?"

Damien and Noriega turned to see three of the
most attractive young ladies standing behind
them.

Trinity had met Angela at Lenore's shop after getting her hair done. They shopped a little, and Trinity decided to go to the game also.

"Trinity, this is my friend Damien and his cousin Noriega. This is my girlfriend Trinity."

"Nice to meet you," they said as they both tried not to stare at her, but it was hard.

Trinity was shorter than Salone and Angela, standing 5' 2, with long, dark, beautiful, healthy hair hanging down her back, cut to a point like a lion's mane. Her skin was flawless—dark and smooth. She wore a white outfit: pants with a draw-string in the waist that was loose that came down just past the knees, and a matching top that came down just below her breasts, leaving her pierced belly button, tight waist and flat stomach exposed. The top was loose enough for comfort, yet snug enough to show her braless, firm C cups. The thong she wore allowed her ass to jiggle with every movement of her body.

Damien and Noriega looked at each other and gave the eyes as if to say, *Only God knows what I'll do to that bitch. Only God knows.*

Noriega walked away and talked to Salone. "We're outta here in a minute."

Damien looked Angela up and down slowly. "Baby, I like—goddamn, baby, your nails fuckin' me up; I like that shit." He smiled.

"I was hopin' you would."

"I got something that's goin' to set that shit off." Damien reached over, getting the two wrapped boxes off the table. She opened one. He reached inside and pulled out a diamond tennis bracelet. The gold glittered as it went on her left arm. The other box contained a nice gold chain that now brought some well-deserved attention to her slim neckline.

By this time Noriega and Salone had returned. Noriega handed Damien another slim box. He opened it and took out the gold Movado watch and placed it on Angela's right wrist. She stood there shocked, heart racing with happiness.

"That's real nice, Damien. I hope you taking good care of my girl," Trinity said. "She couldn't stop talking about you."

"Shut up, girl . . . tellin' my business."

"I hope she can't. Now I know I'm on her mind too." He and Noriega looked at the ladies walking out the door, looked at each other, and shook their heads, knowing their girls were nice. But Trinity's shit was tight—that shit that would make a niggah dig in his pocket quick. All was said without a word.

Damien smiled and focused his attention back to Angela walking out the door. *Damn, she phat as hell. I know muthafuckas goin' be tryin' to holla.* He slapped her ass to let her know that those new Calvin Klein's were fitting—and because he could. She slapped his hand and leaned into him. He put his arm around her waist and their lips met. Then their eyes. So many words were said in a split second. And they got in the truck and were out.

Chapter Twelve

After the game Angela went out to her father's house to spend the rest of the weekend. Trinity stayed with her so they could talk and catch up on old times.

Trinity asked Angela, "So did you enjoy the game?"

"Hell, yeah. Anytime Hampton beats Howard, it's a glorious day."

Trinity turned on the radio. "You crazy as hell, girl. I see your daddy still got his little girl's room sitting here."

"I'm still his baby girl," Angela said without thinking; "you know how they are."

Trinity, whose father was never there, grabbed her bag. "Naw, I don't, but I'll survive."

Angela started looking around, then went in the closet and pulled out a small fan. "Girl, I need something to blow this smoke out." Angela lifted the window and set the fan in a position to blow the weed smoke out the window. Then she threw a towel down at the door and rolled up a Back and

lit it. She inhaled and passed it to Trinity, who
turned her down.

"You wouldn't have to go through all that if you
fucked with this—" Trinity pulled out a small bag
of coke.

"Naw, bitch, you do you." Angela pulled on the
Back a little harder, allowing the smoke to fog her
mind. She had seen girls and guys starting to fuck
with that shit out the way, but it wasn't for her—
weed and liquor were her only desire.

"I was goin' to ask you how you been keepin' the
weight off, but now I see."

"You crazy, girl. I just started fuckin' with this
about six months ago. I got my shape back when
shit got tight as hell and school was almost a thing
of the past. I was around here having a hard-ass
time. Then 'you know who' got locked the fuck
up, and then I was really fucked. Then one day I
was out walking, trying to deal with my frustrations
and some niggahs rode up on me, and guess what
they said and did?"

"What?"

"Now I'm at the lowest point in my life, Angela."
Trinity's eyes started to water. "And they rolled up
three deep in a Cadillac—new shit, girl—and two
of them held out about three grand in each hand
and said, 'Bitch, you got some big titties and a big
ass—if you toned it up and lost that belly, I would
give you three grand just for you to dance. Might
give you five to fuck. But guess what, this is all you
get until . . .' and that niggah threw a hundred on
the fuckin' ground and they peeled off laughin'."

"What you do?"

"Picked up that hundred, bought my baby some
food and shit, and took the rest and joined a gym.

Got in there and met this girl. She'd seen me in there for about two weeks and told me if I kept it up, I could get a job with her. We became close and she started bein' my personal trainer. Within three months I was looking like this. And within four months I was dancing like this." She stripped, removing her top and skirt, and began dancing.

Angela, high and shocked at Trinity's new life, sat staring at her girl's every move. *Damn, this bitch got skills like the girls I seen on TV.*

"Dancing pays all right up here, but I go to DC or Baltimore and do private shows and I get that three thousand. Them niggahs said it, and now I do it. I'm straight, my baby straight. I'm still in school and I even got money to put on the books for 'you know who.' And all he got to say to me is, 'Who you fuckin' for money?'"

"Who are you fuckin' for money?"

"I ain't had no dick since that niggah got locked. One day I'm gonna tell him that it ain't the niggahs you got to worry about—it's these pussy-eatin' bitches."

Angela stood up. "What!"

"Don't knock my thing. You do you, and I'll do me . . . like you said."

Angela frowned. "Girl, you lost me."

"Like I said, Angela, it was the lowest time in my life and she just came in, being my friend. Then we got close and one night it just happened. Only thing is, she always do me and will never let me touch her."

"Bitch just eat your pussy?"

"Yeah, I just lay there and she does shit to my body no man has ever done or can do. Afterwards, sometimes I feel funny, but I enjoy it when it's happening. I enjoy her when she's around, and when I get horny, I look forward to her doing her thing. I know I can't fall in love with no bitch, but I can't see no other niggah—except for Tite—runnin' up in me, skeetin' all in me and all over my sheets. So until he comes home, and only God knows when that will be, I'm goin' to play on the other side of the water."

"I'll stick with dick, girl. I will stick with the dick." Angela handed Trinity a shirt.

"Yeah, but you can get some of this money, girl; you got the body for it."

"I work. I got my peoples, and Damien handles his."

"You just said it—*his.* Girl, you better get his and whoever else's you can get, because niggahs just want to get their dick wet. Please tell me you got another niggah and you ain't open on this non-talkin', knotty-head-ass, Jamaican niggah."

"Girl, you know I keeps me two, three danglin'." Angela laughed and gave Trinity five. "Got a niggah name Mac. Fine, real estate muthafucka with dough—couple-hundred-thousand-dollar-home dough. Ain't gave him no pussy yet, but I felt that niggah dick layin' all on my thigh, beggin' to get in. I controls my shit—don't get it fucked up." They gave each other five and laid there in silence.

It was noon and Damien was headed out to get Angela. Noriega wanted Damien to stick around and check out his business deals. He and Salone were going to Chicago to check on a club venture, and he wanted Damien in on it and to bring Angela along. But with school and work, that wouldn't be possible. Damien talked about the possibilities, but gave no definite answer.

After a little while, Damien was on his way to get Angela and head back to Norfolk with a new business venture on his mind. After arriving at the condo and taking in all her bags, he decided to break out. She had work to do before class and some shit to tell Monica about the weekend.

That evening Angela and Monica were looking at the *Jamie Foxx Show,* eating popcorn and sipping Alizé when the phone rang. "It's Mac," Monica said, covering up the phone. "He's been callin' all weekend."

Angela came to the phone. "Hello. How are you?"

"I'm fine. How was your weekend?"

"Fine. Just did a little shoppin' with my dad and step-moms. I always have a great time in Maryland."

"If it's not too late, I would love to stop by and see you."

She wasn't really up for company, but it had been quite a few days. "Sure, I'll be here."

"Is he coming over?"

"Yeah, for a few. I'm not going to be up late."

"Yeah, yeah! Now finish tellin' me about his cousin."

"Girl, the niggah is fine. Real dark and jet-black, wavy hair, with real pretty skin. Gots plenty dough— baby is paid," she said with excitement in her voice.

"Do he have a girl?" Monica asked.

"Yeah, and she's very attractive. Look like a fuckin' model. Slim like a model. But you can tell her shit is tight. Bitch from France, but went to Howard. She a together girl; I like her.

"Damn, the good ones always got a bitch in the cut. Don't matter . . . she better keep his ass up there because I still wouldn't mind meetin' him. Shit, I got a man."

"Never know. He might just come this way . . . you never know."

Then a knocking disturbed the girls' conversation.

"I'm going to bed," Monica said. "I'll see you in the morning."

Chapter Thirteen

Mac came in and sat down with Angela. They sipped Alizé and talked until the late hours. He wanted to stay with Angela, but she didn't think it would be a good idea. After explaining to her that he really missed her company, all he wanted was her next to him to hold in his arms. That would definitely make his night. She finally agreed and they went in her room and went to sleep.

The running shower woke Mac. He wanted to make love to her so bad. All night long, every time she brushed against him, it made his body cry for hers. After she came out of the bathroom fully dressed, he got up to wash his face. She walked over and hugged him. She couldn't resist; he looked like a Greek god, standing there in his silk bikini drawers. Her body moistened as she felt his dick rise for the occasion when he pulled her close to him. She wanted him and last night it took all she had not to give in. In his arms she felt so secure, so overpowered, she wished he would have been a little more forceful and had just taken her, instead of always coming across like the perfect gentlemen.

"So will I see you later?" she asked.

"I'll do my best. I have an appointment that I know will run until late, but I really want to spend more time with you, so I am going to do my best." He headed for the door.

It was now November and the last couple months had flown by, and being with Angela had been glorious. Mac had never met anyone like her. He couldn't explain the feeling he got when she was in his company, but inside he knew she was the one. And the excitement that came out of her when she was introduced to something new made him long for the opportunity to show her the world. He pulled the French doors open that allowed him to step outside of the master bedroom and stood on the balcony of his two-story brick home, staring out over his covered pool while the brisk breeze came across his face. It was a week before Thanksgiving and Angela had invited him to have dinner with her parents at their home.

He turned and walked back inside. He moved closer to the bed, staring down at the two empty condom packages. Then he focused his attention to Angela's bare body lying on his California King. He and Angela had shared many special evenings, but last night was special.

He sat down on the bed and rubbed her back, reminiscing about the night before and how he could hear the smile in her voice when he told her the limousine was coming to pick her up at seven. When the limo arrived she was to get the wrapped gift box out the back and it would be her attire for the evening. He had personally gone out and bought her a navy blue, velvet evening dress by Carol Little.

The limousine then took her to his home in Lafayette Shores. When she walked in, he had the mellow sounds of Najee playing throughout the house as the chefs and servers waited on them. He wanted Angela to feel like royalty in his castle; to be served a gourmet dinner prepared by one of the finest chefs in Hampton Roads. He'd brought several dozens of roses, red and white. He had rose pedals sprinkled from the front door to the bedroom and on top of the hot water that filled his Jacuzzi.

After dinner they slow danced. As their bodies intertwined, he felt something. Something different. He picked her up and carried her to his room. He slowly undressed her and took her hand to guide her to the Jacuzzi where he bathed, and then made slow passionate love to her. He started at a slow pace, but with the condom on and the water, he could barely feel her wetness, but he kept going until he was dripping sweat in the hot, steaming water. He moved her to the bed and dried her off, taking the massage oil that he'd purchased from Victoria Secret and slowly began applying it to her body. She allowed him to take every toe and finger into his wet mouth, before he buried his face into her vagina. He took in her every move, her every sound, and fell in love with the sounds and her love noises. He lifted himself and climbed on top of her. He entered her and didn't last fifteen minutes before he found himself climaxing, even with the condom.

He had to get her home so she wouldn't be late for class. When he pulled in front of her condo, she said, "Last night was beautiful. I've never been treated so special. Thank you." Nervous the other might happen to pull up, she never felt comfortable sitting in front talking with Mac or Damien.

"Close the door a minute," he said. "Have you ever been skiing?"

"Once . . . when I was eleven." She remembered when Dr. Statton took her and her mom to Masanutten.

"During the Thanksgiving holidays, I would like you to accompany me on a ski *slash* business trip. Some business, but more recreation."

"Sounds exciting. I would love to." She leaned over and kissed him and proceeded to get out the car. *Damn, a ski trip sounds exciting and romantic.*

One more day of this shit and then my vacation begins, Angela thought as she turned in her test paper. She wondered if Damien was going to help her study. *He could be so helpful sometimes.* She remembered how helpful he was the other night. He was supposed to meet her at the condo when she got off.

When she arrived, him and Monica were inside smoking, with Tupac blasting out the speakers. They all sat watching *Moesha, and Malcolm and Eddie,* getting lifted before deciding to order Chinese food.

As Angela and Damien went into her room, she was feeling tired and groggy. He decided to help her wake up and, boy, did he wake her up. They did their thing and showered. When they came out, he sat up with her, drilling the material into her head.

Angela was walking across campus on her way to take her final exam when she felt somebody's arm wrap around her.

"Heah, baby," Rome said.

"What's up?"

"Not a thing. Just ready for the weekend."

"I know what you mean. I'm going skiing and plan to have a ball."

"With your family?"

"No, me and my friend, Mac. He has a condo at a resort, and we're spending the weekend in Colorado."

"Enjoy yourself but be careful; I don't want to see you hurt. I'll see y'all tomorrow night. I'm coming through," he said, running off to holler at another girl.

Angela continued across campus to the bookstore in the plaza when she saw Damien's truck parked at the Burger King. She didn't want to go over by the truck and see him talking to another girl—that would really fuck up her day—but she couldn't see that happening. She walked over to where he was and Damien was sitting on the passenger side talking to a girl standing outside the truck. She stood there in her tight Levi jeans, black Nine West boots, short black leather and long micro braids.

The girl's real cute, Angela thought. She could feel the jealousy rising in her. She knew how bitches were and she knew Damien. *He was a catch—he carried himself well and had that phat-ass truck—any 'ho' be glad to get their hooks into him.*

She made her way over to the truck. The young lady turned and looked at her. Damien turned to see who the girl was staring down and saw Angela standing there with a look in her eyes to cut.

"Can I talk with you?" she asked in a sharp tone, not being too polite.

"Yeah, hold on." He turned to finish his conversation.

Angela never moved. She just stared into the truck at Damien.

"Look, it was nice meeting you," Damien said to the girl as she walked away. Then he got out of the truck.

Angela watched as his winter-green Timbs hit the pavement and he stood in front of her with his green Phat Farm hoody.

"What's your fuckin' problem, Angela?"

"Why you out here with that bitch all in your face . . . like you just don't have no respect for me?"

"My brother stopped over here, and she came to

the truck and started talkin' . . . not that I have to explain myself."

She started to say something.

"Shut up! I don't have time for this jealous shit." She put her hand up to his face. "Whatever."

He grabbed her left arm and took a firm hold of her chin with his right hand. Then he pushed her against the truck, putting himself up against her so she couldn't move. "You know who you fuckin' with—I'll split your muthafuckin' skull and not think 'bout it. I'm not the one. You better get your shit right. Now carry your ass to class or home." He pushed her and got back in the truck.

She walked back to her car with tears in her eyes. "I don't have to put up with this shit," she yelled as she headed back into the Hampton Tunnel. "He didn't have to grab me—simple-ass muthafuckin' Jamaican. I need a real man anyway, not a drug-dealin' punk. Fuck you!" She yelled coming out the tunnel onto the bridge. She had told her mother she was going to stop by but decided instead to get herself together and go straight to work.

She was at work hating him, but every time the phone rang, she wished it was him. It seemed like the longest four hours, and he still hadn't called.

The phone rang again. "Hello. Robinson, Madison, Fulton, and Williams."

"Hello, Angela. It's Mac. How's your day goin'?"

"Fine. Just tired, and my day still not finished."

"Thought I might see you later," he said.

"I'm kind of tired, but I'll call you when I get home."

She stopped by her moms before going home and got there just in time for dinner.

"I know you're going to eat."

"No, I'm not really hungry."

"Sit down and eat something. I don't care if it's a piece of corn bread, but you have to eat something," her mother said, fixing her a plate.

They sat down and started to bless the food. Her little brother was holding her hand, squeezing it and playing. She looked at him and smiled. *You're something*, she thought.

"Amen," they said together when the prayer ended.

"You know I want you here early Thursday to help out. Your friend still comin'?" her mother asked.

"Yes. He asked me to go to a ski resort with him this weekend. Business and fun."

"I don't agree, but you have to make your own decisions now. Where is it anyway?"

"Colorado Mountains," Angela said low.

Her mom looked at Ken. Ken just looked at her. He knew Thursday's dinner was going to be very interesting.

The next morning Angela got up in a foul mood. Here she was, getting ready for a long weekend in Aspen, and she wasn't excited. (Mac had come over the night before and showed her pictures of his deluxe, picture-perfect, mountainside condo in Snowmass Village.)

She went to her only class of the day to take a test. She scrambled to stay focused, but her mind kept wandering off, thinking about what she was going to say to Damien or how she was going to say it. She strolled around with a knot in her stomach that was keeping her from even thinking about eating. All she wanted was to be in Damien's arms again and for things to be back to normal. Eventually, she buckled down, finished her test, then went home.

When she arrived, she found Mac sitting in front of her house. She forgot she told him she only had one class that morning. Angela really cared for Mac and enjoyed his company to no end, but he wasn't who she wanted to see.

"Hello, Angela." He opened her car door so she could get out.

"Hello, Mac. How you doin' today?"

"I'm okay."

"Mac, I don't mean any harm—nor do I have anything to hide—but I don't like unexpected visits. I would rather you call before coming over. I make my mother call and she pays the rent, feel me?"

Mac had a confused look on his face. "I don't see the problem."

"There isn't a problem," she said in a soft, sweet voice, "but next time, please call first."

"Okay, I'll hit you up first, if that's what you want."

They walked inside while he talked about how excited he was about the weekend and how good it was going to be to see the guys from his fraternity and investment group.

"I came by because we need to go to Ski World and get my baby prepared for the slopes."

Angela put her things up and they headed out

the door. She listened to him talk about the great
time they had the previous year.

As he ran down the scenario, he noticed she was
in another world. "Are you all right, Angela?"

"Yes, I'm fine; I just have a few things on my
mind." Angela felt she could open up and discuss
anything with Mac—he wasn't just somebody to
fuck; he was her friend. But being on the outs with
Damien was bringing her down, and she had to
figure out a way to deal with it.

They arrived at Ski World and she began brows-
ing at the skis, ski suits, hats, goggles. Together
they picked out the necessary things and she tried
them on to be safe. They had the counter filled,
she couldn't believe the total. This is when she realized how expensive the sport was.

She watched to see if Mac was going to pull out
the fat knot like Damien, but he reached in his
wallet and threw down his gold VISA credit card.
He didn't even have fifty dollars cash in his
pocket.

"So is there anything else you need?"

"Long johns."

He smiled. "Thermals."

"Whatever."

"Let's go by Coliseum Mall. Then I can drop
this offer off on this house that I received today."

By the time Mac was dropping her off that
evening, she saw the familiar cars in the front.
Then she spotted Monica and Rome holding bags
from The Package Store. They gave her a hand
with her bags. Her and Mac said their good-byes,
and he was out.

"What the hell is all this shit?" Rome asked.

"My girl goin' to Aspen," Monica told him. "Bitch goin' to hit the slopes."

"You ballin', ain't you, shorty?" Rome asked. "Got a niggah with a LX 450 Lexus and then this niggah pulling up with the big-boy 500." He grinned. "Wonder I can't get on."

"And poor-ass Ray just couldn't cut it when it came to the major players," Monica said.

"It's not even like that, y'all."

"Bullshit. Who the fuck you think we are? You and Monica both know that if them niggahs ain't have no paper you'd still be fuckin' with Ray boy. His brother told me and Joe you wrote that niggah a Dear John letter while he was away—that shit wa'n' even right."

"It ain't your fuckin' business anyway, Rome," Angela said opening the door.

"I don't give a fuck. I'm going to speak my mind. You don't run shit here. Fuck I look like—one of those yes-niggahs you fuck with?"

"Why you arguin' with Rome, girl . . . actin' like he yo' goddamn man. Fuck him."

"Naw, fuck both of y'all niggahs. Better straighten out *your* act."

When they walked in the living room, Angela realized that they had other company. *Monica and Rome must have already been inside and ran to the store.* She brought the smile back to her face as she greeted everyone. "Hello, everyone," Angela said to Fat Joe, Quinn, and Monica's brother. "What the deal, player?" Angela hugged Monica's brother.

"Nothin' at all, baby. Angela, this is Kim; Kim, Angela." He turned to expose his friend. Angela shook her hand. The girl was tight as shit—nails done, hair done, eyebrows arched, and was wearing an outfit that complemented her body well. Angela didn't expect anything different from him.

She went into her room and laid her things on the bed. She looked at the time on the watch that Damien had brought her, and thoughts of him began to fill her head. The feeling came in the pit of her stomach again. If she didn't straighten things out with him, she wasn't going to be any good to no one. She picked up the phone and dialed.

"Hello, hello."

She tried to catch her voice. "Damien there? This Angela."

"No, he left about an hour ago. Page him; you might catch him."

She hung up quickly and began paging him. She waited three minutes (it seemed more like fifteen) and paged him again, putting 911 behind her code.

He called back. "What up?" he said, as if he wasn't pressed to talk.

"Where are you?"

"Why?"

"We need to talk." All she heard was silence. "Please, come by for a minute, so I can talk with you. Please . . ."

Angela was sitting in the front talking with her company when a knock came at the door.

Monica opened the door, and he caught eyes as he came in. "Let me take your coat," she said.

He handed her the big, puffy, "bear" coat, which matched his bear boots.

Angela looked at her niggah and smiled. She knew her man was always styled to impress. She looked him up and down, from his Pelle Pelle jeans to his Pelle Pelle shirt with Marc Buchanan down the sleeve. The long chain that hung down on his stomach let muthafuckas know he wasn't from VA—that was some Up-Top shit niggahs was on.

"This is Dee, everyone. These are all my friends, and that's Monica's brother and his friend, Kim."

Kim stood up smiling, and they embraced. "How you been, Dee?" She shook her head like, *I know your name.* "It's been a while."

"I'm straight, and you? What you doin' here?"

"I go to school at Virginia State. You have to come check me out." Then she hugged him again, and they continued talking.

Angela looked at Monica.

When Dee broke away, Angela walked to her room and gave him the eye to follow. She closed the door. "How do you know her?"

"She from Up Top. Her peoples live on same block; we go way back."

"She act like y'all real close like that."

"Actually, we just knew each other from Up Top, but two years ago I was in Richmond for a minute and chilled with her and her girl. We all became real tight, but that's history. "What's up?"

Their talk soon escalated to an intense discussion. That's when Damien threw up his hands and said, "I have to go." He came out and got his coat and asked Kim to walk him down so she could get his number. Kim came back about twenty minutes later.

Angela looked as if she had an attitude with the world. Damien had her fucked up, and she wasn't in the mood for anything. She went into her room, as her company sat around getting fucked up, playing cards, looking at the Wayans brothers.

"Is she okay?" Kim asked.

"She'll be a'ight," Monica said. "Just upset."

Kim got a blunt and walked over and knocked on Angela's door. Angela was lying across the bed, her eyes red with despair.

Kim sat down beside her. "Can I talk to you girl-to-girl?" She lit the blunt. "I know Damien from way back. He was always a wild-ass niggah. Niggahs was shook when he came around; plus, his peoples were known to wild out." She passed the blunt.

Angela sat listening, soaking in all the inside shit on her man. To her this was a dream—somebody just telling his story.

"What I'm about to tell you is between you and me. Never mention it, please . . . because he'll hate me and it will fuck up the relationship I have with him."

"Promise. I'm just tryin' to learn this niggah."

"Damien grew up fast, just like all the other kids on our block—everybody chasin' the dollar bill. Most of the guys who started hustlin' either ended up gettin' got, or in jail. Somehow, Damien and his cousin—I forgot his name, black-ass, fine niggah . . . Well, anyway, they blew up in the hood.

"Once he had money, every girl out our way wanted to fuck him, and he had his share. Then he met my cousin Annette. They kicked it for a while and then she left for school—Virginia State. He decided to move to Richmond. I came to Virginia State and was going to stay on campus, but he and my cousin insisted I stay with them. She kept accusin' him of fuckin' around all the time, but then one day he came back early from a trip to New York and walked in on Annette fuckin' two scrub-ass niggahs that he was sellin' to."

"Fuck he do?" Angela passed the blunt.

"Nothin'. He left and went to New York. About a month later, they were all at McDonald's on Broad; regular hangout. Him and his cousin pulled up and started blastin'. Four niggahs got killed, and my cousin got caught in the crossfire. That was the last I'd seen of him. After all this happened, I was sittin' home about a week later and Damien's cousin came to me and let me keep the car, saying that he'd paid it off. He gave me money for my rent for two years.

"I know they never meant to kill Annette so I never blamed them; I blamed it on her lifestyle. Damien told me that whenever a girl start accusin' him, this pops back into his head and he sees another problem. He knows how it feels to be betrayed, so when you start trippin' and accusin', you push him away. I could tell by his conversation he cares about you, and I will tell you you will not find a better man. But you have to trust him and put some faith into him. And I promise you that niggah will be all that and more." Kim threw her hand up for a high five.

"Thank you," Angela said, and they hugged each other and went out to join the fun.

Angela could now see why her jealousy got that

niggah hot. She knew she'd talk with him, but not until after the holiday weekend. She prepared herself for the days to come. *It was going to be great*, she thought. *A very romantic weekend with Mac.* However, she still had to get through the next day's dinner.

Thanksgiving dinner took a turn for the better. Angela's mom's biggest concern was Mac's age. She even went as far as asking Mac what his interest was and why he was dating such a young girl. Mac kept his poise and explained that when he and Angela met his intention was strictly a friend-to-friend relationship, but over the weeks they had become much closer. Now, he just wanted her to enjoy some of the finer things in life that he'd been enjoying by himself for so long.

He won over Angela's mom, but Ken wasn't so easy. Ken let it be known that Mac was too old and had games up his sleeve that Angela's head was not ready for. "She needs to talk to someone closer to her age," Ken argued. And going away so far with this guy was out of the question in his book. But deep down he knew her mother would have the last say so because Angela wasn't his daughter.

Before the end of the night, Mac and Angela had Ken and her moms behind closed doors in a big disagreement. Ken never even came out to say good-bye.

"He doesn't believe in this trip," she said, returning to the den. "Mac, my daughter's safety is in your hands, and please bring her back the same way you leave here with her."

"I promise you I will; you have nothing to worry about."

"Mom, I'll be okay; don't worry."

"I know. Just be careful and be smart. I love you." Then she held her daughter in a tight embrace, as if it was her last time holding her.

Chapter Fourteen

"That was a'ight. I'm glad you called and invited me."

"I'm glad you here," Salone said. "Noriega seems like a different person when you're here."

"He does seem to smile a little more," Gwynn added. "He's usually very direct and hardly ever talks, but I saw a different Noriega today."

"So, Gwynn, how long you been living in DC?" Damien asked.

"About three years. After going to school in the East, I decided to go back to California and finish graduate school. After I received my master's from UCLA, I knew the East Coast was where I really wanted to be, so here I am."

"So have you regretted your decision in any way?"

"Not really. I left a good man in Los Angeles, but he didn't want to leave. We tried a long-distance relationship that lasted six months before I called and his new girl answered the phone. You know how the rest goes."

"I've been there, but you can't let a bad relationship keep you down." Salone excused herself and went upstairs to see what Noriega was doing."

"I haven't let anything keep me down. I jumped into my work and let it take over my life. I've grown from an administrative clerk for different political organizations, to a job in the Pentagon. I've dreamed of the life I live right now; nothing could make it better."

"So you have a new man, someone to come home to every night? A niggah sittin' in the crib, waiting for you to come home so he can massage your feet, wash your back, and hold you through these cold-ass nights in DC?" Damien walked over and poured himself a glass of Rémy XO.

Gwynn looked at Damien as he fixed his drink. *Damn, he's a good-looking guy,* but she felt he was too young.

It was just a few months before she turned thirty. She'd been in DC for three years and hadn't dated anyone, except for the white Congressman who owned the condo under hers. She and Salone had been friends for a while, and seeing neither one of them really hung out, they both put a lot of time into their work. But Salone came home to a strong black man every night, while she sat alone in her lavish two-story condo.

"No, I don't have a man in my life doin' those things, but I'm all right."

"Then you lied to me . . . because something could make it better—I could make it better." He smiled as he took a sip of his drink and stared into her eyes. He had just met this woman today and was feeling her.

"I didn't lie; I'm contented with my life, Damien. I don't need a man to make my life complete."

"I know you don't, but when you leave, I would like to see how you live, go over and keep you company. That a'ight?"

"Why?"

"Because I want to spend some time with you. Maybe I'll massage your feet or even wash your back."

"What?" she asked, even though she'd heard him.

Damien smiled. "Nothin'."

Just then Salone came downstairs. "We're going to play Scattergories. You ever played, Damien?" Salone set up the game.

"No, but I'm with it. Willin' to learn." Damien looked at Gwynn. "You goin' to teach me what you know?"

She just looked at him and smiled. "You're too much." Then she said to herself, "Maybe I need to consider showin' you where I stay."

Noriega caught the last of the comment. "Goddamn! How long I been upstairs, Salone? Dee making moves on our guest and shit."

They played card games until the wee hours then Gwynn and Damien broke out.

The next morning Damien was on his way back to Norfolk. He drove down Interstate 64 listening to Notorious B.I.G., and as "One More Chance" played, he thought about the video and remembered how he used to ball in the club, him and his peoples, buying out the bar. Then as the chorus came in, *Biggie, give me one more chance . . .*

His thoughts went to Angela. He was upset with her for the way she played herself out at the school, but he missed her. He'd had a good time with Gwynn but wasn't pressed on what she had to offer. If he was broke and needed the help of a woman, he would've looked at her in a different way. But he had plenty dough—*fuck what a bitch had*. He knew he had to be happy and that's what Angela brought to the table.

He forgot he'd told her that he was going to New York, so he figured it would be better to wait until Sunday and give her a call. Then he could have Saturday to himself, maybe go to Pizzazz. If he ran into her, he could tell her he just got back. Here he was trying to figure out how he would explain shit to her and they were on the outs. He'd never had to explain himself to no girl. *What the fuck?*

He leaned over and removed the CD from the deck. "I Don't Want To Be A Player" by Joe was playing on 103 JAMZ. He listened to the words and remembered how he used to be. Now, Angela was the only thing on his mind. It was then he realized that he loved her.

"It's freezin' out here, Mac. Where's the car?"

"Right here." He opened the door to the Mitsubishi Montero Sport, and they climbed in.

Angela had her hands between her legs, trying to get warm, and the cold leather seats were not helping. She looked over the snow-covered land and took in the beauty of it all.

Mac couldn't find a black radio station, so he threw the Mary J CD into the changer. While rolling to their destination, Mac pointed out different landmarks to her and, at the same time, tried to give her pointers about being on the slopes.

"This is Snowmass Village." Mac came to a stop. "Welcome to my winter getaway." Mac had a slight smile. He knew this shit had her mesmerized.

Angela stared in amazement. She never figured this place would be so beautiful. It was lit up, bright and beautiful. It reminded her of Waterside, downtown Norfolk, but instead of restaurants and clubs, this was a resort. It wasn't just the building, but also the snow that covered the open windows, window seals, the grounds and the mountains that left her speechless.

"Here we are, baby," Mac said, opening the door to the condo.

"Oh my God!" She dropped her bag at the door and walked around slowly, looking at the white leather furniture, with the base that held the glass tables, and the fireplace that was already burning with a bearskin rug lying in front of it. She walked into the bedrooms—two master suites with king-size beds—and the view could not be put in words. "I have to get a picture . . . because there's no way I could ever explain this to my peoples."

Mac reached in his bag, took out his camera, and began snapping.

Angela was like the perfect model, standing in front of the fireplace, lying on the rug, standing in the windowsills, holding two bottles of champagne

and allowing Mac to snap away as if he was a professional photographer. She was never going to
forget this.

"I have a meeting later on. Then I have a short
meeting Sunday before we leave, but all the other
time is ours—you and I, baby." He took her into
his arms and laid her on the bed. He'd been wanting to take her in his arms since they were on the
plane.

She was feeling him and wanted him just as bad
as he wanted her. She had the picture in her mind
of him laying her on the bearskin rug and making
love to her until she begged him to stop.

He undressed her slowly and stepped back, as if
her beauty stunned him. She lay there watching
him undress. He removed his T-shirt and leaned
over and kissed her. Then he reached down and
removed his shorts and guided his hard, throb-
bing dick inside her.

"Where's your condom?" She jumped up as if
he'd burned her with something.

"I forgot them, and plus I feel it's time we
started trusting each other. You are mine, Angela,
and I love you. You not going nowhere and neither am I—I'm done with those things."

*This niggah think I'm that caught up in the fuckin
moment.* "What about me gettin' pregnant, Mac?"

"I'm not going to cum in you, girl. I ain't tryin'
to go there." He held his hard dick in his left hand
and reached for her with the right.

"No, Mac, I'm not ready to take the chance."

"I would have to go to the store, Angela. I
promise I won't. Put your trust in me this one
time," Mac pleaded; "don't spoil the moment."

"No, I can't see it. I'm feelin' you, but I can't, baby."

"Fuck it, I'm not goin' out now," he said, getting dressed.

She ignored him and reached in her bag and pulled out her thermals, slid on a T-shirt and relaxed in front of the fireplace.

He put on his clothes and left.

She sat there wondering what he was thinking. She had never been with any man without a condom, except for Damien. She didn't even know why she allowed him, but he had somehow gained her trust and, over the months, never came in her. She turned on some music and poured herself a shot of Rémy. She didn't care if they made love or not, she was relaxing and enjoying herself.

Her mind drifted to Damien. Since she had started fucking him he would be romantic sometimes and set the mood; other times he would be *like I want you right now,* pull her to him, lift skirt, pull down pants, whatever. He would take charge and fuck her like a wild dog in heat. And she actually liked that, never knowing what to expect.

Mac came in hours later running to change. "You can go get you something to eat; I'm going to be tied up for a couple hours," was all he said before going out the door. She walked downstairs to the restaurant and got a bite to eat then returned to the room to wait on Mac. She sat staring out the window, wishing like hell she had some weed. *If Damien was here, I would be a high as bitch and wouldn't give a fuck what we did, if anything at all.*

* * *

Mac came in and got himself a drink. He sat beside her on the couch. "You ready to hit the slopes?"

"It's all on you, baby." She tried to soften him up, not wanting the vacation to sour.

"I'm sorry about earlier, I just wanted you so bad and the thought of stopping fucked my head up. I hope you're not too upset at my action."

She walked over to him and straddled him in her panties and T-shirt. "You have condoms now, and I'm not upset."

Mac lifted her straight up and laid her on the bearskin rug. He lifted her T-shirt and began massaging her breasts as he ran his tongue across her nipples. He took off her shirt and pulled her panties down and stood back staring at her body glistening from the firelight. *Goddamn, this girl's body is a fuckin' dream. I will never let this shit go. She will be mine.* He undressed again, laid down beside her, and pulled her on top of him so he could stare into her eyes and enjoy her beauty.

He gently put his hands on her hips and moved her like he wanted her to move. She relaxed and let him guide her until she saw his eyes close and his body extend. He squeezed her hips, and she kept moving her inexperienced body back and forth. Then his body began to jolt, like he was having a seizure.

She enjoyed the gentleness that he shared and the tenderness when they made love. He was so attentive, but she had never cum with him. Only during oral sex.

He laid there exhausted. She sat on top of him, waiting for him to get up, flip her over, and fuck her until sweat dripped and her pussy squeezed at his dick for more. But he wasn't Damien—being aggressive and rough wasn't him, yet she wouldn't mind if he fucked her correctly.

Within an hour they were on the slopes. Angela was definitely an amateur, but with Mac's skills and help, she was skiing like a novelist by the end of the evening. Later they sat in the windowsills, sipping on Baileys and coffee, looking at the snow that fell slowly on the slopes and trees. She stood up and made herself comfortable between Mac's legs. He hugged her and kissed her neck. She was all he wanted; the woman he loved.

They got dressed and walked down for dinner, joining four other couples that they'd skied with earlier. They had soups, lobster, and steak, and popped bottles of Dom with dinner. Mac's friends all had money and mostly discussed their next meeting, arguing about where it was going to be. After dinner they all sat around the fireplace, drinking champagne and sharing lies, and everyone was having a great time. Especially Angela. She'd finally fallen into the groove of these old heads. But she wasn't used to the champagne, and it wasn't long before Mac was taking her to the room and calling it a night.

When Angela woke up the following morning, Mac had already gotten out to attend his meeting and finish up his business with his colleagues. After his return they hit the slopes again, did some last-minute socializing, and headed back to the room.

"This was a great weekend, but it ended too fast. I really enjoyed this, and I really like skiing.

"We'll come again, baby. Real soon."

Chapter Fifteen

They arrived at the Norfolk International Airport that evening, got into Mac's Benz that was left at the airport, and he took Angela home. She threw her things on the couch and collapsed. "How was it, girl?" Monica was ready to hear every juicy detail.

"Light a blunt, bitch, and I'll tell you everything—startin' with this niggah wantin' to run up in a bitch 'raw dog.' "

"Oh shit! Talk to me, girl." Monica lit the blunt. She couldn't understand how her girl made it the entire weekend without smoking. "Did you take any pictures?"

"Yeah, but they won't be ready until tomorrow. We have to go to Wal-Mart about noon. I'll probably pick them up before I go to work." Monica passed the blunt to Angela and she took a long drag. The smoke went down the wrong pipe, and she began choking, but quickly got herself together. "Monica—I almost forgot—Tuesday, I want to go see your doctor and get on the pill or talk to someone about that shot shit you get every couple months . . . something."

"No problem, girlfriend. How much sex y'all have while trapped in snow? I know you two got mad busy."

"Actually, we only fucked twice. I didn't cum all weekend, but I still had a ball."

"Is the niggah that weak, girl? All he got is the Benz—rich-ass niggah with no fuck power." Monica wasn't smiling.

"He gots rhythm, but he just acts like he can only dance to one song. Damien, now, he's the muthafuckin' deejay and he keeps goin', and goin', and goin'."

"Just like the energizer bunny."

"Just like he got batteries in his ass. By the way, did my baby call?"

"No, but I saw him in Pizzazz Saturday, lookin' fine as hell, rockin' Versace shit, bitches all in his face."

"He see you?"

"We talked for about twenty minutes. He bought drinks and shit, but he never asked about you. Didn't even mention you."

Angela sat confused and heartbroken. She cared for Mac and enjoyed his company, but she loved Damien and wanted him to be her man, all hers.

The week was going fast. It was already Wednesday, and she hadn't heard from Damien. She had paged him several times and even called his house, but there was no response.

Meanwhile, Mac was calling everyday, but he was working and wasn't trying to see her until the weekend.

But she wanted to hear from Damien. She couldn't take it anymore, so when she left work she went by his house. He wasn't there so she taped the letter she had written at work to his door. She had to get a response. All she wanted to do was tell him sorry and then fuck until he begged her to stop.

The next night, she and Monica were looking at *New York Undercover* when the phone rang. They looked at the caller ID. "It's not coming up," Monica said.

Angela jumped up to answer the phone. "Maybe it's Damien." It happened to be Quinn calling from Richmond. He and Monica talked awhile then said their good-byes.

After the conversation with Quinn, Angela went in her room and laid across her bed, listening to the quiet storm. She kept beating herself in the head for wilding out on Damien. She started picturing Damien fucking the girl by the truck. The girl was cute and her face was plastered in Angela's head. Angela was feeling sick. She wanted to get up and just go ride by his house and see if his truck was there. She tried to fight the knot that was balling in her stomach. She climbed under the covers and fought to hold the tears back. At that moment nothing in the world mattered.

Just as she was beginning to doze off, the phone rang. She knew it was for Monica so she never bothered to get it. After the fifth ring she reached over and picked it up. "Hello," she said, not even trying to get her composure.

"What up, baby?" The island accent brought her to her feet.

She had so much to say and didn't know how much time she had, so she decided to talk fast. But when she opened her mouth, she couldn't put it together. "I'm sorry, Damien. I am. I just felt like I had gotten stabbed in the heart and I let it get the best of me. I'm sorry, baby. Please understand." Then out of nowhere, "You said I was yours and you were never letting me go," and she burst out crying.

"Shut up, Angela. That shit is yesterday, and today, my love, is a new day. So shut the hell up with that shit." He said it like it was nothing.

"I'm just coming back from Up Top. I'm coming through the Hampton Tunnel right now. You going home with me, or you want me to call you when I get home?"

He could have gone down Route 1 and across the Chesapeake Bridge, but he'd been missing the shit out of her, and this would put him right at her front door. He had business to keep him occupied through the ordeal, but lessons had been learned and it was time to "dead this shit."

"Yes, I'm waiting in the doorway. Hurry the hell up, please." She hung up the phone without giving him a chance to respond.

Monica opened her door and saw her throwing on her sweats, T-shirt and Reeboks. "Where you goin', girl?" Monica figured it had to be Damien. She could see her girl had been crying, but the happiness that sat on her face was slowly erasing the tracks of any tears.

"That was Damien; he on his way," Angela said through a thousand smiles.

"You weren't this excited when you were on your way to Aspen—you really care for this niggah, huh?"

"Girl, this week has been hell. I been tryin' to get through this bitch. When I was in Aspen, I felt he was tryin' to find me, so I was able to keep goin', figurin' I had the upper hand . . . that he was chasing me. But when I got back and he hadn't called, then you saw him and he didn't even ask about a bitch, I've been fucked up ever since. I don't think I ate three times this week." She walked over to her girl and stared her in the face. "I care for Mac; I love Damien. I love him, Monica. He gives me a feeling that . . . I can't explain it." Angel hugged her girl.

"Go hug your man, then kiss your man, then fuck the hell out your man and let him realize what he been missin' for the last week. Don't forget what Biggie said, girl: *If they head right, Biggie there every night.*"

They both laughed. Then they heard the bass from Damien's truck.

"See you tomorrow, girl," Angela said.

"Be careful, Angela. Love you, girl." They smiled at each other as Monica watched her girl until she reached the truck.

Damien jumped out the truck, and she fell into his arms. He hugged her like he didn't want to let her go. They jumped in the truck and headed to his house.

"Heard you was in the club Saturday."

"Yeah, just had to get out for a second, you know? Where the fuck you was?"

"At my mom's. I've been there since Thanksgiving. How was your Thanksgiving?"

"Fine. I spent it with Noriega and Salone."

"That's it? Just you three?"

"No, she had a girlfriend over." Damien said it like it wa'n' shit, knowing her mind would wander.

A streak of jealousy shot through Angela, but she instantly caught herself, realizing if she wasn't on the outs with him, she probably would have been in DC.

They arrived at his house and walked through the door. As soon as he sat the things down, he pulled her to him and threw his tongue in her mouth. She placed both arms around his neck and sucked his tongue. Damien threw both hands in her sweats and palmed her ass. In one quick motion they fell against the wall, and he pushed her panties and sweats down to the floor. He slid off the clothes and sneakers as her body lay pinned against the wall, then he grabbed her left leg, lifted it and threw his wet tongue across her clit.

She jumped. Then as he buried his tongue into her pussy; she relaxed her head back on the wall. He licked and sucked as the juices ran down his chin. He never thought about stopping because the sounds that she made pushed him. When she was pushed over the edge, she let out a soft scream, gripped both sides of his head with her hands, and allowed her body to fall into ecstasy and fold into him. Before her body was re-energized, she found herself "on the steps," raw dick entering her from the back. She tried to move with his every movement until he began to speed up and fuck like a wild horse. The harder he went, the wetter she got. His body began to shake and jolt, then he collapsed on top of her back.

* * *

The next morning when Angela woke up, it was too late to even try to make it to class. She went to the bathroom and showered. When she returned Damien was staring out the window. "Those are for you." He pointed at the two boxes on the dresser. "When I was Up Top I was thinking of you, and this is to say that I really care."

She opened the boxes to find a 2ct diamond baguette bracelet and three Greek key bangles. She saw the diamonds in the bracelet and could only imagine what it cost. She'd seen the bangles in the shop in DC and they ran a thousand dollars apiece. She walked over and hugged him. "This is beautiful, and I don't know how to say thank you. Words aren't enough."

"Words along with your actions is all that need to be said. Just continue to show me love. I'm not use to really expressin' myself, but just take my actions as a way of sayin' how I feel."

"Is this saying that you love me?"

"Not exactly, but it's sayin' that I really do care," Damien said as he walked to the shower.

He came from the bathroom hype, as if the shower had given him life. "What you gonna do today?"

"Whatever. I have a hair and nail appointment tomorrow afternoon." She knew she couldn't keep going to DC to get her shit done, so she decided to give Monica's hair stylist a try.

"I have some friends that I do business with that's comin' in town tonight. We supposed to meet for drinks later, so you're goin' to have to run home and get some clothes. Now is good, then we can come back and just do nothin'." Damien began to think about the thirty-minute drive and corrected himself. "Why don't we just go to Greenbriar Mall and get you some shit for today?"

"Either way, Damien, house or mall, I can find something both places." She smiled.

In the mall Damien saw two girls with fly, short cuts. "Them bitches got they shit cut like yours."

"You right. I need to ask who did they shit. At least I can say I seen the girl work, instead of just takin' a chance."

"Ask 'em."

Angela hesitated, so Damien yelled out and the girls came back. After introducing Angela as his girl, he asked where they got their hair done.

"The House of Rica on Granby Street," said one of the girls.

"Ask for Fred," said the other. "He's high as hell, but he's the fuckin' bomb."

After coming out the mall, Angela called to see if she could get in, but he was booked solid. "The soonest I could get you in is next Friday," Fred said.

Angela figured the wait would be worth it. After talking with him, she remembered him from her church and realized he had the reputation for being the shit, not only with the hair, but also designing and sewing.

* * *

Mac was upset. He'd been calling for a week and kept missing Angela. Monica told her that sometimes he was calling first thing in the morning and that he realized she hadn't been staying at the condo. Monica added, "He even stopped by one evening and was questioning me about your car being here and you wasn't."

That's when Angela pulled up. They got into a heated discussion about her now-so-busy schedule, when actually Damien was getting all her time.

Damien had dropped Angela at the hair salon after getting her nails done. When she finished, he was sitting in the parking lot, waiting for her to come out. He wanted to ask her to go to Jamaica with him, but he knew she had school and he would be gone at least a week. She came out of the salon and got in the truck. He always examined his girl from head to toe every time he saw her. He noticed the new outfit and all her jewelry. He noticed the 1ct Marquise diamond baguette ring that matched the bracelet he'd bought. And the new Michael Anthony diamond watch that he knew he didn't buy. "Nice watch and ring."

"Thanks. My mom and dad gave it to me," she. said without looking at him.

(The other evening Mac took her out for dinner at the *La Galleria* on Great Neck Road for dinner. As usual they were dressed for business, and when he picked her up, he came with flowers and gifts. Those were the gifts. She just forgot to leave them at home.)

She kept talking to get his mind off the jewelry, but his conversation was short and direct. She could tell something was wrong. She continued to talk until they arrived at her condo. "When are you coming back?" she asked.

"Next week. I'll call you from the island. Angela, look—I'm not one to act like the jealous kid, and this has nothin' to do with jealousy, but I will let you know that I'm not comfortable with your gifts."

"I told you my parents gave this to me."

"Look, I'm not sayin' you're lyin', but your parents never gave you expensive gifts like that before. That's a hell of a place to start. Do you know what that ring and watch cost?"

"No." She wondered where he was going. "It was a gift."

"The same way you don't know what those bracelets cost that I gave you. Angela, I'm going to say this and then I'm done with it—that ring cost almost as much as those bangles, and all three bangles cost over three grand."

Her eyes widened.

"That watch cost almost as much as that bracelet, and it ran fifteen hundred. Now you say your parents bought it, but if they didn't, anybody buyin' gifts like this will come to light. All I can say is—don't get caught in the crossfire; it's a dangerous place to be." Damien looked deep into her eyes as he spoke. He left wishing she was telling the truth, but knew she wasn't. *Whatever she's doin' in the dark will come to light.*

Angela walked into the house knowing she had slipped. She had been seeing both Mac and Damien for almost four months and, with their complicated schedules, it was going fine. But she never wanted

Damien to get suspicious; he was her love. But she enjoyed Mac's company also.

Angela saw Monica at the door with her bag. "Where you goin'?"

"Girl, I told you I was going to Petersburg this weekend to see Quinn."

"Yeah, that's right. You have a safe trip." Angela hugged her girl.

"You better be safe." Monica knew how crazy guys could get, and her friend didn't know the game like that.

"Girl, I'm okay. Damien just left headed for the islands and Mac will be here at nine. We gonna look at the entire *Godfather* tonight. I was going over his house, but since I got the house to myself, I guess I'll chill the fuck out."

They said their good-byes, and she lit the blunt, trying to get her head right before Mac arrived. Then she heard a knock at the door and, thinking Monica had forgotten something, she opened it, wearing nothing but her panties and opened blouse. She was shocked to see Ray standing there. He grabbed her and pulled her close.

She gave him a half-hug and pulled back, holding her blouse together.

"No need to hide it," Ray said smiling; "I've seen it all before. How you?"

"I'm fine." Angela stared at Ray. *The Marines had turned him into a man,* she thought. He was clean-shaven just like Mac, but had lost the boyish look. The baby fat was gone; he had bulked up, showing his now cut physique. He had on sweats and a T-shirt that read *USMC* across the front.

"When did you get home?"

"Just came in and I wanted to drop off this and let you know that I'm going to stop through later so we can sit and talk. I got to go now; I'll see you later." Staring at her, he kissed her cheek and handed her a box. She looked better than when he left—the makeup, the nails, and the beautiful jewelry she wore made her look like those fly-ass bitches that he always thought was all about money. Money he didn't have. But he still felt that he had Angela and that they just had to talk.

Angela opened the box after Ray left. He had bought her an 18" Figaro chain. She sat it on the counter to give back to him. She knew it didn't cost much. *It's the thought that counts.* He looked good, but he wasn't her interest and she had to return it. All she had to offer to him was her friendship.

Mac arrived about nine thirty. She opened the door to see him dressed in a suede suit by Dolce and Gabbana, some crocodile-skin boots, and holding two pizza boxes. He handed her the pizzas.

"Make yourself comfortable."

He kicked off his boots and laid his suede coat across the barstool.

"I see you decided to go back and get them."

"Yeah," he smiled, "I figured I'd treat myself to an early Christmas."

Angela walked over and took his hand. He had on a stainless steel Rolex on one arm, a platinum 5ct diamond baguette bracelet, and a platinum 2ct diamond ring. She stared at Mac thinking he was that man any woman would want. She remembered the day she saw the jewels at the jewelry store in Hilltop, an exclusive shopping area in Virginia Beach. He'd walked into one of the jewelry stores and each piece that he'd looked at cost over eight thousand dollars. Made her wonder just how much money he had. At this moment this niggah was shining and that shit had her going. "Treat yourself well, huh?"

"If I don't, who will? But I still got plenty love for you, and I will always treat you just as good—believe that." He smiled and shook his head up and down, staring at her.

"I heard that! And the answer to your question—*I'll* treat you good. Maybe not to that extent, but to the best of my ability." Her voice was soft and sweet.

"I know you will, love. I know you will."

Mac pulled the *Godfather* sagas from the Blockbuster bag, and she sat down beside him to enjoy the pizza and the movie. As the evening progressed she relaxed in Mac's arms. Her only worry was she didn't want Ray to come back. She fell asleep in his arms until the late hours, and they went into her room and climbed in bed.

The following morning Angela was awakened by Mac's soft, wide lips on her neck. She snuggled her ass against his dick. He was just kissing her, but she wanted some. He kept kissing her back as his hands roamed across her breast. Her nipples hardened. He reached over, pulled the condom out his pocket and slid it on. She lifted her leg, and he grabbed his dick and slid inside entering from the back.

He began stroking slowly. *This bitch ain't tight as she was in Aspen—like she been fuckin'. Or is it because she so wet?* His mind began to wonder as his pace speeded. He couldn't picture her fucking another niggah, but it was fucking with him.

He didn't stop until he finally came. He laid there holding her, with thoughts bouncing off his brain. Finally he realized that he couldn't worry about simple shit like a kid. *If she was fuckin' up, it will come to light.* "I'm goin' home to shower and change. You want to go to Williamsburg?" Mac asked getting dressed.

"I'll be waiting." She got out of bed to go over and rub his chest.

He sat his shirt down and hugged her beautiful, naked body when the loud knock disturbed them. Her stomach dropped and began to churn. She walked over and threw on a T-shirt. *Please let it be somebody sellin' something, please God.* She walked out to the front door while Mac stood in her doorway in just his boots and pants.

Angela opened the door and there was Ray standing in the doorway. He stepped in as Mac was putting on his wife-beater. Ray had seen the Benz in Monica's spot, but he didn't want to believe that another niggah was in the crib with Angela.

"What you doin' here, Ray? It's just a little past ten." Angela asked as if Ray was just a friend, hoping he would follow after he saw she had company.

"I have to have a reason to come see my girl."

Angela's breathing quickened at his response and her stomach tightened when Mac's hand touched her shoulder and pulled her back to him.

"So who did you say you were, partner?" Mac asked real calm as if he really wanted to hear it again.

This can't be happening, Angela thought.

Ray said, "I'm her boyfriend—who the fuck are you?"

"What's goin' on, Angela?" Mac asked. "You need to talk to your little friend?"

"Yeah, Angela, do you need to talk to your little friend?" Ray spoke in a little squeaky voice imitating Mac. "Need to carry yo' ass with that gay shit."

"You need to chill, partner. And, Angela, you need to start talking before both of y'all get fucked up in here." Mac's voice was cool and calm, but his insides were boiling. *The dark was coming to the light and this bitch better start talking.*

Angela's churning stomach went away when she heard Mac's comment. Angela moved Mac's hand from her shoulder. "Who you think you gonna fuck up?"

Mac turned to her with a surprised look. *She got this niggah hollerin' she his girl and gonna get smart because I asked her to explain. This bitch playin' me for soft.*

Then, all Angela saw was darkness. The unexpected open-hand slap to her face buckled her knees. Mac jumped back and caught Ray in the jaw, but the punch never affected Ray. Mac began to throw a flurry of blows at Ray, but Ray kept coming until he went down, scooped Mac up by his legs, and slammed him to the floor.

Angela was screaming for them to stop. Mac

scuffled to his feet still throwing blows to get Ray off of him. When Ray tried to slam Mac again, Mac waited for him to bend down and quickly stepped back and kicked him on the side of his head, which sent him slamming into the wall. Several blows to Ray's head sent him to the floor. He balled up in a knot, trying to fend off the kicks and punches.

Angela ran over and grabbed Mac when she saw the blood pouring from Ray's head. Ray saw the light of the open door and scrambled out on his knees and began running down the stairs, leaving nothing but a trail of blood.

Mac slammed the door when he saw Ray scurrying out of the parking lot. He turned to Angela, who was standing there crying. "Fuck that cryin' shit. You gonna play me in front of that niggah. I ask you something and you gonna get smart." Mac came towards her. "You think I'm one of your fuckin' buddies or something," were his last words before she felt the blow to her forehead. It sent her over the back of the couch. Before she could hit the floor, he grabbed her by her neck and with both hands, lifted her little body off the ground. Her feet were swaying back and forth as her breathing was slowly being cut off. "You wanna be smart? Be smart now. You wanna play? No bitch plays Mac." He threw her through her room door, and she fell to the ground in tears.

She was no longer feeling the pain of his abuse, she was too scared. She jumped up and dove across the bed to her phone and tried to dial 911. She had only gotten to dial the 9 when she felt something go across her back that stopped her every move. She tried to scream but nothing came out. She thought he had drawn blood, but it was his crocodile belt he'd snatched off and took across her back.

"Mac, I'm sorry. I'm sorry. I won't do it again, I promise." Angela tried to get away.

He grabbed her by the T-shirt, twisted it in his left hand, and pulled it until her arms were extended over her head. Then he pushed her head and neck into the bed and pinned her down. She fought but couldn't move. Like a helpless child he beat her naked ass with the belt until she stopped fighting.

Angela cried like a baby. "I won't do it no more! I had written him a letter; he's my ex-boyfriend! My ex!"

The belt continued across her butt and legs. She had given up, thinking the torture would never end. Then it did. He grabbed the back of her neck and pushed her face into the pillow. "Don't you ever—I mean, ever—turn against me. You belong to me, and don't ever put the next muthafucka before me. Do you understand?"

Mac stepped back, put on his belt, and grabbed his shirt. "Maybe you need some time to yourself." Mac stared at her on the bed, balled up, shaking, and crying. He felt proud of himself. He knew that he loved her and this was going to make for a smooth relationship. He had put his foot down and let this young girl know who she was fuckin' with.

He left her on her bed crying hysterically from the pain and in tears from fear. For hours she couldn't move. She was feeling as if all her security had been ripped away.

* * *

When Monica came in later that evening she saw the wrecked house and dried blood on the wall. "Oh my God." She ran to Angela's room. Angela was lying covered up and still shaking. Monica went over and touched her. When she pulled back the cover and saw the welts that ran from her girlfriend's back to her thighs, she let out a scream. Tears began to form in her eyes. She picked up the phone to call Angela's parents.

"No, don't call my house."

"Then I'm callin' the police. Who did this—that sorry-ass Jamaican? Those muthafuckas think they can do what the fuck they want. I never liked his muthafuckin' ass anyway."

"It was Mac," Angela said crying.

Monica looked at her in amazement, like she couldn't believe what she'd just heard. "Fuck that shit! He gots to pay for this shit, one way or another." She dialed 911.

The police arrived, took a report, and demanded Angela go to the nearest hospital. While at DePaul, two other officers were called in by the doctor. They picked Mac up at his home in Lafayette Shores.

While being held downtown he attempted to call Angela several times. Monica denied all his collect calls. She finally accepted one. "What the hell could you possibly want, son of a bitch?"

"Put Angela on the phone."

"What the hell she got to talk to you about? Something is wrong with your ass."

"Fuck you! You tell her when I get out—" was all he got out when Monica hung up on him.

"You need to get a restraining order against that niggah—he really crazy."

"What was he yellin'?"

"Something about when he gets out, but you know he's not coming by here."

The phone rang again. They thought it was Mac but realized it was coming from Ray.

"What the fuck do you want?"

"I need to speak to Angela."

"No, you don't. Your punk ass started all this shit. Then you ran your bitch ass off while she stayed here fightin' your battles. Don't call here no goddamn more, boy." Monica slammed the phone.

"You need to tell your parents."

"No, then my mom be actin' all funny and shit. I'll handle it. I'm gonna go to court, and he'll pay for this shit." Angela was scared and kept thinking about the five minutes of horror that was threatening to turn into a lifelong nightmare.

On Monday Angela was still in no mood for school. The incident really had her nerves fucked up. She never thought a man in his right mind could do that to a woman. Especially not the ones she picked. *At least the police would straighten him out.* She was standing in the kitchen washing up dishes when the phone rang. She picked it up expecting Damien.

"Baby, I need to talk to you."

"I have nothin' to say, Mac; I just want you to stay away."

Mac could hear the tension in her voice. "Look,

Angela, I let them bitches get in your ear. Listen—
and I'm goin' to say this one time—you are mine.
If you act like a child, I'm goin' to whip your ass
like one. I hope you remember. Now cut out the
bullshit."

"Stay away, or I'll call the police."

"Fuck the police! I got one of the top attorneys
in the state on retainer. Think I give a damn about
the police?"

Then she heard the knock at the door. She was
glad somebody was going to be there with her. She
opened the door and there stood Mac. She tried
to close the door, but little force on his part got
him inside. He grabbed her from the back and
hugged her. "Relax, relax, *r-e-l-a-x*," he said slowly.
"Baby, I love you; I wouldn't do anything to hurt
you."

"You already have, Mac. After all this, I just want
you to let me go. Just leave before you get into
more trouble."

"What you goin' to do—call the man again? You
can call then, soon as I get out, I'm comin' back.
This shit can go on forever . . . because you will be
with me. Who's gonna give up first, huh?" He
eased her over to the sink. He held her with his
left arm and, with the palm of his hand, cocked
back and slammed it into the back of her head,
forcing her face into the dishwater. The force
slammed her teeth into her tongue, and pain shot
through her mouth, now filled with dishwater. She
never saw it coming. Terror shot through her
body. He lifted her head, still having a firm grip on
her neck. "Now, who's your fuckin' man?" he
asked; his mouth pressed against her ear.

She was scared, confused, and didn't know what to do. "You are, Mac . . . you're my man." Her voice trembled with fear.

This turned him on. Just last week she had him so fucked up and emotional, but now he was in control. She felt him reach down to unbuckle his belt. The fear of what she'd gone through gave her a burst of energy. She spun around, bringing her elbow across his face, knocking his head back far enough for him to loosen his grip. She began kicking and throwing blows, fighting for dear life.

He was out of control. The quick punch to her chest left her gasping for air. She dropped to her knees, but her every hope was snatched from her body when she felt the brown, leather belt wrap tight around her neck and snatch her to her feet. "Please, Mac," Angela cried, "I love you, baby. I do. Don't do this." Angela tried to get her hands between the belt and her neck, but the more she tried, the tighter it got.

Mac guided her body against the wall. He twisted the belt around his hand and was pushing her around by her neck. "Show me some love, Angela. Show me some love." He pressed his body against her ass, undid his pants, and let it drop to the floor. "Get those tights off and open up," he said real calm.

"Mac, I'm beggin' you . . . let's go in the room. Not like this. I'm not goin' to fight you."

Her begging turned him on. He stood behind her poking her butt with his hard dick. "Angela, listen carefully—if I got to tell you one more time, I am going to rip that extension cord off the blender, drag you into the bathroom by your neck, strip you down, throw you in the shower, and fuck you up royally. Try me!"

Her prayer for Monica to come home or for anybody to knock at the door went unanswered. She leaned down and removed her tights, opened her legs, and elevated her ass.

Mac was full of smiles as he entered her, never letting go of his firm grip on the belt wrapped around her neck. "How you feel, baby? How you feel?" he asked, slowly sliding in and out of her.

A blank expression on her face, Angela fought back every tear. "Good, baby. Good."

Mac's pace increased as he moved closer. He pressed her against the wall, dug his fingers into her stomach, and pounded in and out of her like a wild animal. She felt the release of the belt on her neck and felt his body shut down as he came inside her. "Did you enjoy it, baby?" Mac removed the belt from around her neck and acted as if nothing was wrong or different.

She stood motionless, in a daze and staring straight ahead, the side of her face still pressed against the wall.

"Angela, I love you, and nothin' is goin' to keep me away. But you better believe if you try and lock me up again, I'll be back—on campus, at work, here. I'm not sure where I'll catch you, but I will. And, I promise you, your family won't be able to recognize the remains. Don't ever go against me, baby. I really hope you understand. Now I'll call you later." He leaned over, kissed her on the cheek, then walked out the door.

Angela stood in the kitchen with her pants laying beside her, barely able to move, with cum running down her leg. She began crying, wondering what the hell she had gotten into. *No man in his right mind would act like this, and the police couldn't do shit. And if the police couldn't do shit, then my parents wouldn't be able to do a fuckin' thing either.* She made her way to the bathroom and fell in the shower, allowing the water to run on her body until there was no more hot water. She threw on her robe and laid across the bed.

The phone began to ring. She wanted Monica to come home. "Yeah," she said with no strength or enthusiasm.

"It's Ray; we need to talk."

"No, we don't; I'm done, just like the letter said."

"Angela, we were happy. I know things didn't change like that in a few months. Has it changed? Do you love that niggah, or what?"

"You'll never understand. Don't call or come here again, or I'll change my number," were her last words before hanging up. She felt nothing but hate and resentment for Ray and Mac. Even her only good thoughts for Damien were slowly fading away, figuring it was just a matter of time before that fantasy life fell through.

The last week had been hell and torture and Angela saw no way out. She needed a friend, a male companion, strictly for his friendship and had no one.

The phone rang again. Angela started not to answer it but prayed it was Monica on her way home. Monica wanted to see how her girl was doing since she had to go to the library and would be late coming in. Angela tried to handle the situation by not thinking about it, but her ordeals were heavy on her mind, she had been violated and controlled. *And this muthafucka feels he can do it whenever, like I belong to him.*

She walked to the front and turned on the TV. Sitting in the room she felt as if she was going to lose her mind. She was looking at "In the House" when she heard a loud knock at the door. The knock scared her to death as she balled up on the couch. *That door was not getting opened until Monica came home.* The knocking continued. Then she heard a familiar voice. She eased to the door. "Who is it?"

"Open the door, girl," Rome said. "What the hell you doin'?"

She opened the door. Rome saw a look that he hadn't seen on Angela's face since he'd known her. He walked inside and shut the door. Her back was turned to him. "What the deal, girl?" Rome walked up behind her.

She turned to him and fell in his arms and began crying. He waited for her to calm down and asked again.

"Nothin'."

"Look, Angela, don't tell me nothin'. I know you and this ain't you. Now what's going on? You know me and you know I don't fuck with nobody but my brother . . . so your shit is between me and you. Understand?" Rome sat her on the couch.

"Rome, right now I just can't talk about it, but I need a friend like you wouldn't believe," she said with tears in her eyes."

"Okay, okay, but you promise to talk to me soon."

"I promise," she said as he put his arms around her and held her. She lay her head on his chest and was fast asleep, feeling "oh, so safe."

Chapter Sixteen

Mac called again and no one answered. He slammed down the phone in anger, not with Angela, but with himself. *She was a great girl, and I fucked up again.* She had shown him nothing but love, and here he was acting like the controlling man his father was when he was coming up. He had seen his father control his mother, his sisters, and his life until he was able to stand alone. He looked around his beautiful home as he poured himself another drink. All the anger he had built up was coming out, and he was striking back in a manner he'd been accustomed to.

He went into his home office and sat at his computer. He leaned back and took the bourbon to the head. "Fuck you, Dad! Fuck you! I have my own shit now. I'm successful now, and I don't need you or your fuckin' approval." Mac screamed at the top of his lungs as he threw books across the room and kicked over the end table. He went to his desk drawer and took out his .45. "Touch me again, muthafucka. Put your muthafuckin' hands on me again and I'll do your ass in." He fell to the floor and went into a tantrum, thinking about the abuse he was a victim of for no reason. So many times his father had made him strip down, get in the tub, and beat him with a leather strap, extension cords, racetrack pieces. Anything that left welts and stung like hell.

Mac remembered all the times his father forced him to eat soap just for speaking out of turn or not saying "excuse me." His father wanted him to be scared of him and he was. Until he reached thirteen and received his brown belt from Curtis Bush karate studio and had won competitions to go to a state championship. When he got there the guy favored his dad in looks and build. Mac stood across from him and saw his father. Without hesitation he almost killed the guy, with all the built-up anger and confusion that was in him. He vowed that the next time his father tried to abuse him in any way, he would stand firm and show him that he was no longer standing for it.

That day had come. His father came into the house after a long day of work and a few beers. He walked into their two-bedroom apartment, where Mac slept on the couch and his sisters shared a room. It was summer and it was hot as hell. He was laying on the couch, trying to catch the hot air that the fan blew around the room. He wasn't really asleep, but acted as if he was to keep from putting up with his dad's nonsense. He heard his father scrambling through the drawer and moments later, felt something go across his back that seemed to cut him deep.

He jumped off the couch, holding his back, listening to his father yell. "Didn't I tell you not to leave water in the goddamn sink? Dumb ass!" As his father raised his hand to swing again, Mac came off with a flying kick that sent his father slamming against the wall. They locked up, and it was then that he realized that his father had come from the school of hard knocks and he was just a pupil.

He took a real beating. His father held his neck in a choke hold until his mother ran out. Mac was gasping for air. All his energy was being drained from his body as he fell to the floor throwing up everything he'd eaten. His father ended up putting him out, so he scrambled in the streets, trying to make it until winter, when he returned home. The abuse never stopped.

Mac layed drunk in the middle of his floor, staring up at the ceiling slowly turning. He stumbled to his feet, sat down in his chair at his desk, and removed his gun from the desk drawer. He stared at the black-handled, squared-off Glock. He put one in the chamber and put the barrel to his head . . . then in his mouth. Mac had tears in his eyes as he contemplated taking his own life. He knew he would never be able to cope with his life's past.

"Damn!" He slammed the gun on his desk. This was the third time he'd been this close to taking his own life in ten years. He reached in the drawer and pulled out a half ounce of cocaine. He poured four grams on the table and made it disappear just as fast. He strolled to his bar and poured another drink. Sitting in his chair with Angela heavily on his mind, he leaned back and drifted off to sleep feeling sorry for himself and Angela. His head was messed up, but he was trying so hard to deal with life and couldn't see living it without Angela.

Angela woke up to the movement of Rome. "Where you goin'? What time is it?"

"Three thirty. I was just trying to get comfortable."

"You can lay across my bed," she said as she headed to her room with Rome following her. They laid across her bed, and she closed her eyes, her mind, and fell into a deep sleep. Neither of them ever said a word.

The morning came fast. Monica got up and saw Angela's door still open. "Get the fuck up—class starts in a few."

Rome jumped up. "Goddamn, I'm runnin' late fuckin' with y'all 'ho's."

"Spark a blunt, niggah, before you run."

"Here." He passed them some weed. "I gots to get to class." Then they heard the door slam.

Monica rolled the blunt and walked in Angela's room. "So how you feelin' today, girl?"

"Fucked up and still scared, but I'm goin' to class."

"Well, at least the welts are gone off your legs."

"Yeah, I'm glad they took pictures or nobody would believe me. But look at my fuckin' neck—that shit hasn't cleared up."

"You'll be all right; that's not that visible. You are a strong one. So what's up? You and Rome buddy-buddy like that."

"No, but he's a real friend; he's mad sweet."

"Yeah, I know." Monica passed the blunt to Angela. "He's very sweet."

After smoking they went to shower. Angela went through her closet. She didn't want to wear anything Mac had bought but noticed that most of her winter shit he'd given her. She pulled out her Liz Claiborne pants suit so she wouldn't have to change for work. The Nine West boots set off the suit, and she was out the door.

When she arrived home later that evening, she came in to find five dozen roses. *Monica must've brought them in when she was home earlier.* She heard a knock and began to panic. She grabbed her Mace from the kitchen drawer. If any foolishness kicked off today she was not going to be overpowered. She put the Mace in one hand and a long knife on the cabinet beside the refrigerator. She opened the door and there was Mac standing there. She knew if she tried to shut him out she would end up like she did the day before, and she wasn't trying to go there. *There's no tellin' what this crazy muthafucka might do.*

Mac walked in, and chills swept through her body. She was scared as hell of this man and trying not to show it. She stared at him, keeping her distance. He was in the kitchen, and she was right by the door, ready to burst out. He stared at her. "I want to explain, Angela . . . I have a lot of problems I'm dealin' with—and that's no excuse for my actions—but I can't change it; all I can do is apologize and promise it will never happen again. I love you like you would never believe, and when that guy said he was your boyfriend and you sided with dude, I lost it. I didn't mean to but I did. And I'm very sorry I hurt you.

"You just don't know how sorry . . . but my jealousy kills every relationship I ever been in and I had told myself not this one, but—" He threw both hands up.

"You say sorry, Mac, but you hurt me. And the trust I had in you is gone. I just don't understand."

"I'm not goin' to talk you to death. I just hope you find it in your heart to give me another chance and to forgive me. I love you.

"I was goin' to carry you shoppin' Saturday and get you some things, but things got out of hand. So here's something to pick up a few things. I'm goin' to give you some space because I know you have some thinkin' to do." He laid two grand down on the counter and left.

Angela still had so much hatred for Mac. She went from being scared to hating him, but as she looked around at the flowers, it softened her. The sight of the hundred-dollar bills made her want to run him down and say, "Fuck your money! Stay away from me!" But when she grabbed the money, she thought out loud, "Damn . . . what a way to say good-bye." *He was dead wrong for all that he'd done and the way he handled his shit, but Ray was the real cause of all this shit.* She saw Mac had a very bad temper and could get real crazy, but the niggah that just left was the niggah she was fascinated by.

Angela clenched the wad of hundreds. "What the fuck?"

"Monica, hold up so I can walk with you." Rome was out of breath from running across campus to catch up.

"Come on, boy. I got to run."

"So what's goin' on with Angela? I've never seen her like this."

"Well, right now she needs a friend, not a niggah tryin' to fuck." Monica gave Rome an uninviting look.

"Shit, what the fuck I look like? I'm tryin' to find out if it was big-ass money with the Lex or cool poppa with the Benz."

"Simple-ass niggah with the Benz. That muthafucka whip Ray ass and sent that bitch-ass niggah runnin'."

"He did what? I guess the Marines can make you look like a man, but if you bitch, you bitch."

"That's not it. After he beat Ray ass and he took off, then that niggah fucked Angela up too. Beat her ass."

The words rolling off her tongue cut Rome. A serious look came over his face. He played and joked with Angela and Monica, but they were his girls and he had mad love for them both. "Know what, man—that shit fucks with me, and if she was my peoples, I would step to that niggah. But she fuckin' that kid and I can't get in that shit; she'll end up hatin' me."

"You right . . . because yesterday I saw flowers and shit that he sent. In a minute I'm gonna start thinkin' Angela like that wild shit. Especially if she keep fuckin' with him after this shit."

"Where's 'Big Money'?"

"In New York, I guess. He'll be back later in the week, but he better stay away. That crazy bitch be done fucked him up too." Monica knew her friend had got herself in a bad situation and felt for her, but quickly realized that all she could do was stand with her, no matter what her decisions were.

Monica arrived at the condo just in time to catch Angela before leaving. She was dressed as if she was going to a business luncheon: the long leather cover, the tight Anne Klein skirt suit she'd picked up on one of her many shopping sprees.

"I know that ain't who I think it is downstairs," Monica said with an attitude.

"Don't start."

"'Don't start? Don't start'? Fuck you mean, Angela? That shit that niggah did ain't normal, and if you let him get away with it he's goin' to end up hurtin' you real bad."

"No, he ain't; I'm just goin' to dinner. He has some things to discuss, so I'm goin' to dinner after work and then I'm comin' home. I'll call you from work."

"Look, Angela . . . Damien will be back soon and then he may come by. Then what? You gonna let Damien walk up on some bullshit like you did Ray so 'Crazy' can beat his ass too."

Angela walked out knowing her girlfriend was right, but she realized that she was caught up. She didn't want to see Mac beat Damien like he did Ray. Ray, she never meant to see him get hurt, but Damien was her real love, and it would hurt her more to see him hurt over her unfaithfulness. She realized that she was going to have to tell Mac it was over, regardless of the outcome.

She came downstairs and Mac was standing outside to open her door. They rode down the street with tension in the air, but as the sounds of *Monica* flowed through the car, her mind began to relax.

"I never knew she sang like that. Her CD is nice."

"My girl got it and this song is the bomb," Angela said.

Mac leaned over and turned the volume up, then relaxed his hand on her leg through the split in her skirt.

She jumped at his touch and looked in his eyes. It was the first time she realized how sneaky his squinnted red eyes looked through the clear Perry Ellis eyewear. She reached down and placed her hand on top of his. It seemed as if she was just returning his affection, but it was to keep his hand in place so he wouldn't be sliding it where he shouldn't. He tried to move his hand, and her grip became tighter. She was beginning to feel uncomfortable. "Relax, Mac, and enjoy the ride."

"What's the problem?"

"No problem; I just want you to chill."

"What you mean 'relax'?" He put his hand back on her leg.

"You really need to stop, Mac . . . like I asked." She tried to remove his hand. His grip tightened on her leg. He grabbed a piece of the skirt and balled it in his hand. "You want me to rip this muthafucka off—I'm talkin' to you?"

"No." She was scared of his reaction. She was trying to be a big girl, but she was really scared of this niggah, who seemed to have two personalities.

He released his grip and rubbed her upper thigh and slid his hand back down to her knee. "As much as my girl turns me on, she don't want me to touch her—what kind of shit is that?" He pulled in front of the lawyer's office. "I don't ever want to hear that shit again. Now you have a nice day, and I'll be back in a few hours to get you; I have a surprise for you at dinner."

Angela got out of the car and walked into the office confused. She didn't know if she was to call the police so he would stay away, or call her mom and get some advice. The police didn't do shit last time and her mom's involvement would just create more aggravation. *Mac definitely ain't scared of the police and there is no way to protect myself from him.*

The situation disturbed her. *How could any man just flip personalities like Mac did?* She didn't know what to do. She picked up the phone to call Monica and straighten everything out with her friend, but to her surprise, Monica told her that Damien had stopped by and was curious why she didn't drive to work.

"What you tell him?"

"That you were hangin' out with your mom and she dropped you off. I think you better call him because he might try and surprise you and pick you up."

"Let me call him; I really don't need to piss him off. That muthafucka was trippin' comin' here, girl, touchin' me and shit. I told him to chill, and he caught a serious attitude.

"What he do?"

"You know how niggahs try to be all rough to intimidate you. He's out of control."

"Well, you better catch up with Damien before he comes up there and Mac do some crazy shit to you and him."

"I know what you mean." Angela hung up the phone and paged Damien.

It was close to the time she got off and her stomach was starting to churn. She called Monica back.

"Did he say he was comin' by here?" Angela asked as soon as Monica answered the phone.

"No, he didn't say, but he insinuated that he might. Oh yeah, he had this black muthafucka with him. Fine as hell, girl."

"Probably his cousin. Look, I'll call you back; the other line ringin'."

"Hello, Madison Robinson Williams and Fulton. May I help you?"

"I'm sure you can if I want you to," Damien said.

"Heah, baby, where are you?" She was so excited to hear his voice but was still troubled with the thought of him coming by and running into Mac.

"I'm on St. Paul's, making a right on Monticello. How were you getting home?"

Before she could answer Mac walked through the door, stood in front of her, and blew a kiss, as if not to disturb her.

"Did you hear me? How you gettin' home?"

"Friend of mine." She was praying he would say okay and change his direction since Monticello was only six blocks away.

"Well, call her and let her know that I got you."

"That won't be necessary."

"Why? What's the problem? Talk to me, Angela."

"I can't right now."

Mac was staring her in the face and realized she was talking to another man.

"Oh, you can't, but you will. I'll see you in a minute." Damien hung up the phone.

Angela hung up the phone slowly, waiting for Mac to say something. "Now I'm just your friend. Can't talk in front of me." Mac assumed it was Ray on the other line. "So you still fuckin' with him?"

"No, it's a friend of mine I hadn't seen in a while and he was stoppin' by to see me." Angela could see the change in his eyes. The same look he had when he hit her before.

"Well, he can see us and talk to us if he's just a friend."

"Please, Mac . . . he's just a friend I haven't seen in a while, so why don't you and I get together another time? I'll call you later, I promise." She was about to cry.

"Hurry and get your shit before one of these lawyers have to read your will. Tryin' to change our plans—bitch, you must be crazy." Mac stared as if he wanted to tear her head off.

She began gathering up her things as he stared with hatred in his eyes. She heard the bass from the truck even before the doors opened. Mac opened the door for her to walk out. She locked the door, and they began to walk to Mac's car just as Damien was coming down the rocky street. He jumped out the truck as they headed to Mac's car. "Let me speak to my friends and then I'm comin'," she said, turning to walk towards Damien.

"If you embarrass me by doin' that, I will embarrass you twice as much." Mac spoke under his breath in a stern tone. It stopped her dead in her tracks. She quickly remembered the last time he hit her.

"What up, girl? What da deal?" Noriega yelled from the truck.

She just waved and focused her attention on Damien walking up. Her stomach turned into a knot as he walked up and hugged her. "What up, baby?"

She gave him a half-hug.

"Yo, Nore," Damien yelled towards the truck, "my girl don't want to hug me in front of her colleagues." Damien assumed Mac was one of the attorneys, seeing he was dressed in the three-button wool suit by Armani.

Noriega jumped out the truck and walked over. Mac stared at him as he listened to the sounds of the new butter Timbs scraping the rocky street.

"Hello, my name is Mac." He said and extended his hand to Damien, and they shook hands.

Mac introduced himself again and held it out towards Noriega.

Noriega left his hand hanging in mid-air and turned to Angela. "So you hangin' out with us tonight?"

"Naw," Mac said, "she's goin' to be hangin' with *me* tonight."

"I'm not talkin' to you, son; I'm talkin' to her." Damien stared into Mac's eyes.

"Well, I answered for her. Now get in the car, Angela." Mac opened the door.

She was scared and confused.

"Look, I don't know what the fuck is goin'

on"—Damien grabbed her hand and pulled her to him—"but you will explain later. Now go get in the truck. Right now." Damien pulled her towards the truck, putting himself between her and Mac.

"Bitch, you tryin' to fuckin' play me." Mac slammed the door and stepped towards Angela.

Before he took a second step, Damien scooped his ass up and slammed him on the hood of his car.

Mac's hands found Damien's throat, but the cold steel against his temple quickly brought him back to his senses.

"*Blodeclaat!* You know who you fuck wit'? No man test me." Noriega let Mac feel the butt of the 9mm, and blood flowed from his head as his body fell to the ground.

Mac saw darkness as he held his head, but kicks from Noriega's Timbs and Damien's Gortex sent his head slamming against the side of the Benz until whimpering sounds came out as he folded up in pain.

"*Moniskunt!* I'll kill ya, ya ever cross me again." Damien's accent was so hard not even Angela could make it out.

"Fuck around and lose you' life, boy." Noriega shook his head as they walked to the truck.

Angela watched the incident, and even though Mac had treated her badly, she still felt no one should get a ass-beating like they had just given him. But for some reason, inside she felt a little relief, even though she didn't know what was in store.

"Hurry up, man. You know I'm on paper," Noriega said. They rode towards Damien's house without a word being spoken.

Angela's stomach was still tight. She didn't know what to expect of Damien once they arrived at his house. She quickly remembered the conversation she'd had with Kim and realized she was riding with two killers. And she was worried that Mac might hurt Damien.

They arrived at the house and went inside and found seats. Damien walked in the kitchen and rolled a Backwoods.

Noriega could tell she really wasn't used to the shit that just went down. "You all right, Angela?"

"I'm okay," she said in a soft, uncertain voice.

"You all right, cousin?" He held his hand out for the Back.

"I'm goin' to be if this girl don't fuck around and make me kill her ass."

"You goin' to be all right. Just talk it out and it's going to be okay. Heah, Angela, what's up with your roommate?" Noriega asked.

"You have to talk to her."

"What's the number?"

Noriega picked up the phone as Angela gave him the number to dial. Angela knew her girl would be glad to hear from him.

The movement of Damien grabbing his coat brought her back to her present situation. "Come on," Damien said, "let's go for a walk." He headed out the door.

They walked in silence for about two minutes before any words were said. "So . . . talk to me, Angela."

"What can I say, Damien?"

He stopped and turned to her. "Look, don't fuck with a niggah and please don't get your shit split playing stupid. I want to know what the fuck is up—and don't lie to me."

She began to explain her relationship with Mac, excluding their trip to Aspen and quite a few other intimate details. She did her best not to lie, to just leave out the things that could get her knocked the hell out.

Damien knew there was more to the story, but the only way he could find out was back at the lawyer's office. And he wasn't about to talk to him. He thought about it and realized he had to do one of two things—let her go and just don't fuck with her no more, or love her the way he'd been doing and hope she learned her lesson.

As they approached the house he looked at her walking with her head down and staring at the street. She looked so innocent in the eyes, so beautiful, but she was so naïve he wanted to take her in his arms and just protect her from the world.

"Damien, I'm sorry. I've made mistakes before, but I really regret this one. I love you more than I could ever explain in words. I just don't want to be hurt."

"Hurt? I travel state to state, making moves, trying to live a comfortable life and, at the same time, trying to make sure my cap don't get peeled or I don't get caught up. Then lately, when I go out of town, no matter what I'm going through, all I do is think about you and getting back so we can be together. It brings a smile to my face and gives me a reason to come here. You're special, but the shit that happened today can't be happening. It could have gotten real bad real quick. Then what?"

She had nothing to say. She was stunned at what she'd just heard. She wanted to hear, "I love you, Angela," so bad, but it never came.

Noriega was on the couch getting lifted when they walked back in the house. The sounds of B.I.G.'s "One More Chance" was pumping through the system.

Damien and Angela looked at each other and smiled.

"Can I have one more chance?" she asked, only moving her lips.

"Hell, no. No more chances here." Damien threw her the keys to his truck. "Look in the back of the truck. It was for you, but now I'm gonna give that shit to Monica."

Angela walked outside and returned carrying two Nordstrom bags. She took a black leather DKNY sports coat out. "Damien, this shit is the bomb." She gave him a hug. She opened the other bag and realized he had picked her up a pair of black boots to match. "Thank you, baby. I love them." She tried them on.

"I guess we crew again, huh, Angela?"

"Be quiet, Noriega." Angela walked in the kitchen. She wanted to get away from that conversation. What she really had on her mind was showing Damien exactly how much she missed him and how much she appreciated him thinking of her while he was away. She eased behind Damien and put her arms around him and rubbed his chest.

He turned to her and kissed her long and slow. "Maybe we need to go upstairs."

Before she could answer, the doorbell rang.

"Open the door for my babe," Noriega said to her.

"Oh, that's your babe." Angela walked to the door, smiling. "What about Salone?"

"We broke up—tell your cousin."

"I was wonderin' why I didn't see her."

"Yeah, right. I heard that."

She opened the door. "What's up, girl?"

"Nothin'—my ass almost got lost. It was light the last time I came out here. So what's going on? Spark it up, my niggahs." Monica sniffed the aroma in the air.

"Here you go, baby." Noriega passed the 'dro rolled in Backwoods.

Monica looked at it and started smoking.

"Monica, your boy told me to open the door for his babe."

"Really? He didn't tell you? We established that earlier." Monica smiled and sat down closer to Noriega than people just meeting would sit. They began to go solo on the Backwoods.

"I'm hungry as shit, cousin, what's up?"

"What you tryin' to eat?" Damien asked, rolling another Back.

"It's all up to you, baby." Angela moved close to Damien.

"What you want?" Noriega stared into Monica's slanted grey eyes. *This bitch is fine as hell.* There was no doubt in his mind that he had to have this. Just the thought was making his dick jump.

Monica had taken off her coat to reveal a tight beige sweater that was cut low in the front, and a black pair of Levi's that looked as if they were painted on.

"Tell me your pleasure, girl, and I'll make it happen. Anything."

Monica stared back at this dark-skinned, wavy-haired, handsome black man. She knew he was talking about restaurants, but wished he would widen the selection. Then she could tell him what would really please her. "I like Pargo's and it's not too far."

"Pargo's it is then, baby. I like your outfit too, girl. All you need is the leather coat, a gold chain to go right there." He rolled his finger from her neck to her cleavage. "It would definitely set shit off."

"You can set shit off anytime you like—I wouldn't be mad at you." They were about two inches apart, talking in codes to each other, but leaving it open to the imagination.

They ended up at Pargo's in Greenbriar. After dinner they sat and had drinks until the restaurant closed. They all left feeling real nice from the blunts and alcohol.

No sooner than they were in the house, Damien rolled some smoke and walked over to where Angela had taken a seat. "I want you bad as hell, come on," he whispered into her ear.

"What you goin' to do, Monica?" Angela asked.

"I'm goin' to spark this with my man, then I'm goin' on home."

"Well, I'll see you in the morning," Angela said, as she and Damien made it up the stairs.

Damien went in the room and took off his boots and T-shirt. He undressed down to his Tommy Hilfilger boxers.

Angela undressed as Damien lit the blunt. He watched while she stripped down to her burgundy bikini panties and grabbed his T-shirt and threw it on. She went and put on the Mary J CD and walked over to the bed.

He stood over her and passed her the L.

She took two long drags and passed it back. As she began to kiss his chest and stomach, he leaned over towards the ashtray and almost dropped it as her mouth eased down on him.

His knees buckled as she began to satisfy him orally. "Goddamn, Angela," he said, his hands massaging her shoulders, "I got to feel you right now baby."

She leaned back and elevated her hips so he could easily remove her panties.

He leaned over and entered her. When he felt himself about to cum, he started to pull out, but her legs locked him in and he came inside of her, collapsing on her shivering body.

Angela rubbed his back. "You okay, baby?"

"I'm fine. Why are you shaking?"

"Why you think? Feelin' you cum inside of me just took me over. I never dreamed it would give me a feeling like this."

"Why did you let me do that?" Damien looked into her face with a serious expression.

"I'm on something now; I got on it for you. I knew pullin' out was gettin' old. I love you, Damien. I really do." Angela got under the covers and laid down as if she was 'sleep.

He lit the Backwoods and laid back. Thinking she was 'sleep, in a very low tone he said, "Girl, I love you too, but I'll never let you know how much."

With her back turned and eyes closed, she smiled,

knowing no other man could make her happy as she was at this moment.

The next morning the rapid ringing of the door-bell woke her up. "Damien, someone's at your door." Angela walked to the window. "It's the UPS truck."

"Go downstairs and sign for it," he said, sleep still in his voice.

When she went to the door she realized her car was still parked. Her girl had decided to stay the night. *Noriega probably begged her to stay.*

She walked in Damien's room and opened the box, thinking it was a gift or something he ordered. She dumped the contents on the bed, and he woke up.

"I told you to sign for it, not open it."

She stood there with her mouth open. She had never seen so much money at one time. She found it strange that it was wrapped in Saran wrap. She watched him count it with quickness and finesse; she could tell it was something he was used to doing.

He handed her twenty hundreds. "Put that in your purse; you will never need nothin' from no-body. If I don't give it to you, then its not meant for you to have. You understand what I'm sayin'?"

"Yes."

"Was my peoples up?"

"No. My car still outside."

"I heard that." *Bitch was all on my cousin dick. She wouldn't have left if he gave her money for a cab.* It didn't surprise him. Since they were young, girls always loved Noriega—even when he was broke. After he got money, he had to beat bitches off.

He walked to the kitchen, and Noriega came out. They gave each other a pound, smiling. Noriega asked, "So what's up, cousin?"

"Not a damn thang," Damien responded. "You tell me, kid. Shit!"

"Young girl got it goin' on; I'll be back down here real soon."

"I wouldn't steer you wrong."

"So what's up with that shit from yesterday? Bitch-ass niggah." Noriega opened up the pack of Backwoods.

"She said it was nothin', that he was an ex that had been buggin' out on her."

"Shit . . . niggahs don't just act up over a bitch unless they fuckin'—don't act like you stupid." Noriega stared Damien in his face.

"Yeah, I know, but people make mistakes. I care for her Nore and I have to give her the benefit of the doubt."

"Look, Dee, she's young and she has to learn, but I can see she got you all open and shit. But I'm not tryin' to see my peoples get in no shit behind no bitch—I don't give a fuck how fine she is. If you love her like that, then you need to stay in her ass. Living like we do, last thing we need is to bring attention to ourselves. You know what I'm sayin'?"

"Yeah, you right."

"A'ight then. Handle that shit like you from Brooklyn, player. You know how we do—BUC! BUC! BUC! Lay a niggah down." Noriega had two fingers extended out like a gun.

"What y'all talkin' about?" Angela asked as her and Monica entered the kitchen.

"Guy talk," Damien told her. "Some things aren't meant for your ears."

"Must be talkin' about us."

"That's another way of tellin' us none of our business," Monica said.

Damien put his arms around Angela. "Never that, baby."

"I was talkin' about y'all." Noriega lit the Back. "I was talkin' mad shit."

"I believe that," Monica said. "Probably tellin' Damien how smooth you were and how you coax me into spendin' the night. But little do you know I knew I was plannin' on stayin' *before* we went out for dinner. You know your black ass too fine and sexy." She rubbed her hands across Noriega's bare chest.

"Oooo," Angela and Damien said as if she had gotten his ass.

Angela watched her friend with Noriega. She could tell she really liked him, but she knew he had a girl.

Even though Monica had a man, he was nothing like Noriega. Quinn was nice and he looked good, but *he* did the chasing; Noriega was fine, nice, secure, spoke with much confidence, and had money that Quinn could only dream of. And if he wanted, he could give her girl anything she thought she wanted.

Angela looked over at Noriega. She could see how her girl could very easily get open over this niggah. They always loved thug-type niggahs. Her mind drifted to Tupac videos and remembered how crazy they used to act whenever they would see him. Damien had tattoos and she found him madd sexy, but Noriega had tattoos on his chest, across his stomach, and both arms, and when he pulled a glass out the cabinet, she noticed that he had "RUDE" on one tricep and "BOY" on the other in Old English letters. His body was sculptured just like Tupac's. She just hoped he didn't end up like the late Tupac.

She knew eventually her girl would catch feelings and be hurt by Noriega, but *that was part of life.* "Niggahs be thinkin' they players and shit," Angela said.

Monica smiled at her. "They don't know we already know."

"I know I'm hungry," Noriega said.

"For real," Angela added.

"I want seafood. Crab legs," Damien said.

"Nothing's open until eleven." Then Monica added, "Let's do this: Let's go to our place so we can change and carry our ass to class. Then we'll come straight back to the condo, where y'all will be waiting, and then we'll go to Red Lobster."

"Sounds good to me," Noriega said. "Then I don't have to be away from my girl too long." He kissed her on the cheek. Then he passed the Back to Damien and went upstairs.

Damien hit it and passed it to Angela and headed upstairs.

The girls kept talking as they finished the half-lit Backwoods.

"Thanks, girl. I'm glad you said that."

"No problem. You know I have to look out for my girl. I know you would be worried about that simple-ass muthafucka comin' over and trippin' after what you said happened yesterday. Goddamn! I wish I could of seen that shit. I would have been hollerin', 'Beat his ass! Beat his bitch ass!'" She could hardly get it out, from her and Angela laughing so hard.

"Do you have to go to work today?"

"I called them and said I needed some study time; they're really understanding."

Talking about Mac brought thoughts of him. Angela knew he had problems and that he was no longer the man for her, but he'd introduced her to several things that would never be forgotten. *One day, maybe, he could be a friend. A very distant friend.*

It was a week before Christmas, and Angela hadn't seen Mac since the incident outside the lawyer's office. He had tried calling, but she refused to talk to him. He even showed up at her door one evening, but without hesitation she dialed 911 and he never stuck around.

Now here she was getting ready to go into the courtroom for the charges she had against him. She had already tried to get the charges dropped so she would be done with him, but new laws changed that "dropping" shit.

As she entered the courthouse and saw him sitting on the bench in front of the courtroom, the hurt and pain that he'd put her through began to resurface.

She tried to ignore the fact that the niggah still looked good in his black slacks, black silk shirt, tie, and sports coat. He was the cleanest brother she'd ever seen. *How could someone so fuckin' fine be so mean and disturbed?* She stopped and their eyes met. She'd forgotten what this man did to her when he stared into her eyes and pulled her close. Mixed emotions ran through her, but her focus was easily snapped back when Monica grabbed her arm. She was so glad her friend had come along so she wouldn't have to face the situation alone.

They sat down and waited for the court doors to open. Moments later she saw an elderly, well-dressed white gentleman come in and take a seat next to Mac.

She thought she had seen this man before— Steve Decker, one of the most powerful lawyers in the Hampton Roads and well respected by judges and prosecutors. She'd seen him meet with lawyers at the firm in which she worked. His reputation preceded him.

After a long session, Mac walked out of the courtroom with a warning, and one stipulation— that he stay clear of Angela.

Steve Decker made the situation seem like a domestic dispute that got a little out of hand, but nothing serious.

Angela was upset because of the lies and projection that his lawyer used to defend Mac, to make her look like a young whore that got caught fucking around on her man. But what else was she to expect? Mac was high on the social ladder and rubbed elbows with big heads throughout the city of Norfolk. He ran in circles with the likes of Ken and his associates.

Growing up in an upper middle-class neighborhood, she'd seen the importance of education and professionalism. Different neighborhood gatherings that her mother and Ken held or attended always opened her eyes to the lifestyle she wanted.

Mac could give her that life and the status. He was someone to be admired by all. On the other hand there was Damien, young and powerful in his own way, and he probably had more money than Ken and Mac. But the way he made her feel could not be compared.

"I know I was told to keep my distance, but I miss you," Mac said as she walked down the courtroom stairs behind Monica.

"The hell with you, Mac. What you did to me and in that courtroom was inexcusable."

Monica told him, "You need to carry your ass before I make a phone call."

"Okay, Angela, I fucked up. I made a big mistake. Do I have to pay for it forever? If you give me the chance, I'll make it up. I never thought being without you would have me so fucked up the way I've been." He eased closer where she could see the water in his eyes. "Please, just allow some time for us to talk. Please?"

Angela began to feel for him. She began to weaken as he preyed on her emotion.

"I'm not goin' to crowd you or try to put you in an awkward situation, but if you find it in you to talk to me, please call. All I ask for is conversation." He walked away.

She walked with Monica in silence. This was the first in a month that she was in a confused state of mind over him. She loved Damien, but Mac was the type of man all her peoples would admire and accept with ease.

"Don't fall for that shit, girl—I know when a niggah ain't shit."

Angela never spoke. *With a fucked up life, who was
she to give advice?* Noriega playin' the shit out of her;
Quinn hadn't been home in months; and Fat Boy
was fuckin' whatever moved.

"What time you plan on comin' back, Angela?"
Angela's mother was frustrated at her daughter's
actions.

Angela continued out the door, ignoring her
mother's calls.

Angela was tired and her head was banging like
she'd been hit in the head with a bat. She got in
her Jetta and quickly drove away. She stopped at
7-Eleven where she could get something to relieve
her migraine. It was cold out, and she never expected to run into anyone, but just as if it was a
hot summer's day, the young thugs that she'd
grown up with were still hanging on the corner,
forties in paper bags and blunts passing from
hand to hand.

As she opened her car door, a pretty new fire-
bird pulled up and parked beside her. A young
man jumped out eager to get her attention.
"Hello, Angela. How are you?"

"I'm fine, Ray. And yourself?" She tried not to
ignore him but didn't really give a damn.

"You lookin' good these days. What you been
doing with yourself? He was hoping she would say
something; giving him an invitation to pursue her
once again. *She's fuckin' gorgeous. Irresistible. Definitely
not the girl I left behind.*

She had transformed into a fly-ass young woman.

He noticed the new-found jewels that rested on her fingers with the freshly designed airbrushed nails. She wore a hat with fur around it that hid her short cut, but brought out every feature in her beautiful face. She'd put on a pound or two, but the extra weight filled the black Parasuco that had her looking phat as hell and leaving nothing to the imagination.

"I've been taking care. Can't and won't complain."

Before he could say anything else, Ski and Quan came walking up from the crowd of niggahs on the corner. "Fuck is up, Angela?" Quan asked.

"Nothin' much. Been a minute," she said, knowing he probably just came home.

Ski yelled, "Angela, drop us off up the street."

Quan opened her back door. "We'll hit you off."

Ray asked Ski, "You don't see me talkin'?"

"Fuck you, niggah. Better carry you' ass. I heard about you." Ski remembered him getting beat down and running. *To lose a fight is one thing, but to let another niggah run you without a gun was the act of a bitch.*

Ray walked in Ski's direction. "Who you talkin' to, son?"

"Yo, Ray," Quan called out, "this ain't the time . . . and I'm not gonna to say it twice."

Ray knew Quan was a young niggah throwing rocks at the penitentiary, that he'd been hustling since middle school and was known for holding heat and having the heart to put something in a mutha-

fucka quick. He walked in the 7-Eleven without another word being spoken.

"So what's up, girl?" Ski asked as they drove
away.

"We suppose to meet Rome. His brother Bo
havin' a party later . . . invitation only. You goin'?
He just bought a fat-ass house with a pool out
Bellamy Woods."

"Yeah, Rome said something to Monica. I
haven't seen him in a minute."

She sat hitting the blunt they had rolled as she
pulled in front of Fat Joe's building.

Rome and Fat Joe pulled up minutes later, just
as she was leaving. He blew the horn for her to
back up then parked and jumped in her car to
talk.

"Almost didn't recognize you. That's your
brother's new car?" Angela asked, referring to the
black GS300 Lexus.

"Naw, that's mine."

"Oh, everybody else doin' it—why not you,
huh? You're being stupid; you have too much to
lose, Rome."

"I'm a'ight."

"I thought you were smarter."

"Look, I don't need the fuckin' lecture," he said
loudly. Then he added softly, "I need a girl who
understands me. You don't care."

"What you mean by that?" She stared at him.

"Ever since that night I stayed with you and held
you, I haven't been able to get you off my mind. I
feel we should spend more time, and you can get
to know the other side of me. But you want to keep
fuckin' with those knucklehead-ass niggahs."

"That's my business, Rome, not yours."

"Fuck that! I'll make it mine and do both those niggahs. Fuck them! Niggahs ain't from around here."

"Listen at this. I don't believe you."

"Yo, shorty, that's how I feel." Rome got out the car. "I never want to see you hurt again, and if you're with me, I'd know you're taken care of.

"Look, my brother's party is tonight, and I want you and Monica to come as my guest. Page me and let me know what's up." He shut the door and left Angela sitting there for a second, wondering what just took place.

Rome was supposed to be like a brother. Where did this come from? She shook her head, smiled, and drove away.

Rome entered the apartment with a serious attitude. "Y'all niggahs finished that package?" he asked Quan and Ski.

"Yeah." Quan handed him fifty-five hundred for the "big eight" he had gotten on consignment.

They counted money, made plans to meet later, and they all left.

Joe had already paid Rome, so all they had to do was go meet Quinn in Richmond and get his. Then he'll be ready to see Bo again. His brother was giving him kilos of "soft" (powder) for 17,000, and he was selling nine for 5,500, which was giving him five grand a week, nowhere near what his brother was getting. Bo was moving five kilos a week; one he gave to Rome.

Rome had learned a lot from his brother. For as

long as he could remember, Bo hustled and made much paper. After the clique he ran with went down a couple years back, Bo became the man. For a while he had to serve out-of-town kids to get back up, because cats in the hood thought he was wearing two faces.

After his clique got locked up, Bo walked away without doing any time. To hear people talk . . . they said that when the Feds scooped him up, he squealed like a bitch against his own man, the niggah that brought him in the game, Lo. The same niggah that took him from poverty to the mainstream. Word on the street was that Lo put a 20,000 mark on Bo, but after two years, it was forgotten about by some. Bo was supposed to be living on the low, but after a period of time he felt he was untouchable. He never really got Lake Edward niggahs in his corner again, so he threw his brother out there, who had built a tight clique. Rome was handling his and making a name for himself.

Rome and Fat Joe were on their way back from Richmond when Rome's pager went off. It was Monica and Angela telling him to pick them up for the party, seeing Damien was in Jamaica and Mac was keeping his distance, but calling the house like a crazed schoolboy begging for love and another chance.

Rome scooped them up, and they headed to the party. Once they arrived they couldn't believe their eyes—on the table in the dining area was a bowl of cocaine, and beside that was a bowl of 'dro for the rolling. Just for company.

Angela noticed there was just as many whites as blacks, but everybody was partying as one. Halfway through the night, Angela was looking for Monica when she entered the back room and saw her girl bent over, snorting lines of coke through a hundred dollar bill that someone had handed her. She looked up.

Angela could barely see her girl's pretty grey eyes.

Monica expanded her hand to give the rolled bill to Angela and signaled for her to do the two lines that were still on the dresser.

Angela thought twice and figured it was the holidays and she was going to have a good time, so she indulged. The coke took her to a new plateau. Feeling refreshed and like they were ready for anything in the world, they partied till the wee hours of the morning.

They woke the next afternoon feeling drained but no side-effects, except for the shits. Angela had gotten a small sack before the night ended. She threw it on the table in front of Monica.

"I guess we know how we startin' this here day," Monica said.

"Shit! You know how the fuck you started the weekend, so keep it poppin', niggah."

It gave the girls a quicker and smoother high than weed. The girls had a new thing.

"That was a hell of a party, kid." Rome pulled shrimp out the refrigerator.

"Bitches were everywhere and ready to serve niggahs with the quickness," Bo said, "and you all in that short face."

"Bitch is bad though, right?" Rome smiled and gave his brother a pound.

"Give it to you, she's nice. But will she pull your back when you really need her?"

"In time she will, son. Promise you that."

"Do your thing, kid. I'm feelin' you. But remember one thing—use them 'ho's before they use you. Them bitches is treacherous." Bo walked to the front door.

Rome watched his brother as he strolled around in his silk boxers and wife-beater. He had always looked up to him because he maintained.

Their older sisters had looked out a little when they were younger, but now they could barely take care of themselves. They were living at home with moms and were headed nowhere. One had two kids and the kid's father was doing five years. The other had three—the oldest child's father got killed hustling; the other was locked; and the youngest kid's father didn't even acknowledge he had a kid.

Bo had always kept his nose clean, except for when he got caught up a while back fucking with that clique that owned that sports bar: Black and them niggahs that were headed for destruction from the beginning. He was now laid back, pulling in mad paper, living like a "Big Willie." But he was not only taking care of himself, but his moms, sisters, and they kids.

He used to take care of Rome, but that was history. Rome was used to having his own and was determined to rise to the status of some of the biggest ballers to ever come out of Bayside, like Tremaine, Big Lloyd, JunePune, Pimp, E, Lo, or, the most notorious of all, Black.

Black was compared to Ninno Brown. He built a name, schooled his little cousin, Lo, and Lo in return schooled Bo. Lo was doing time, and word on the streets was that Black was doing life. Some say that he got caught up in DC and was killed. Rome didn't know what the truth was, but whenever they talked about big-time hustlers that came out of the Hampton Roads, his name was always mentioned.

Rome wanted to make a name. Wherever he ended up in life, he wanted to be known. He wanted ghetto celebrity status, not just neighborhood notoriety. "What you getting into?"

"Go to Lynnhaven. I need to finish up this Christmas shit. Why? You swingin' with me?" Bo asked.

"Yeah, I'll show you the Rolex I want." Rome laughed.

"You get your Rolie when you've paid some fuckin' dues. A Rolie carries a certain amount of respect, and as you know, respect is earned, not just given." Bo stared into Rome's face and gave him a pound. Bo knew Rome was smart, but trouble wasn't him, and in this shit, you had to be ready for both sides.

Rome knew what Bo was talking about—the-other-side-to-this-street shit. He knew Bo had damaged many niggahs during his soldier days and wouldn't hesitate to destroy a niggah today if he had to. He never had to prove himself like that because Bo gave him his start on a platter and the money started flowing. "Ain't shit respected but

this right here." Rome clutched his pocket, showing the knot of money through his jeans.

"Yeah, that do get mad respect." Bo smiled. "You
ain't lyin' there, kid. You ain't lyin' there."

Chapter Seventeen

"Merry Christmas, Sissy. Get up. Come open your present, Sissy. Hurry up!" Angela's little brother yelled.

Angela looked at the clock. It was seven. She knew she was going back to bed. She put on her robe and took her brother's hand. He pulled her to the family room by the brightly lit Christmas tree that was near the fireplace.

Her mother and Ken came into the room. "Merry Christmas, family."

He hugged everyone individually, then collectively. Her brother picked up a present and began to open it. "Hold on," Ken said. "You know we pray and thank God for this day before anything. Now join hands and bow your heads.

"Dear Heavenly Father, the first, the last, the Alpha and the Omega, the one from whom all blessings flow, as we bow our heads on this joyous day, we raise praises for all the good things that you have stored upon us. We stand here as a family, thanking you for the opportunity once again to come together and thank you for your many blessings. We thank you for another Christmas that we all have lived to enjoy the love, happiness, and prosperity that you have supplied upon this family. We cannot thank you enough, but we will continue to give you praises. So we ask you to continue to bless us and watch over us as a family and then individually. We ask this of you in Your Holy Name."

They all said, "Amen," and began opening the gifts they'd bought for each other.

Angela eased to the kitchen and called her father. She hadn't spent a Christmas with her father since her parents got divorced. She missed her dad at times like these. Even though Ken always did all he could to make the holidays a family thing, no matter how sweet he was, he still couldn't take the place of her father.

After talking to her dad and Lenore and wishing them a Merry Christmas, her spirits were lifted and this precious day was off to a great start. They were listening to Christmas music and sipping hot chocolate. Ken was enjoying a cup of coffee mixed with several shots of Baileys.

A knock at the door disturbed the family.

"Angela," Ken yelled from the foyer.

Angela walked out, and to her surprise, Mac was standing there, looking gorgeous as ever, with a gift in hand. She wanted her step-dad to excuse them so she wouldn't have all her business out.

"What are you doing here?"

"I came to see you, baby. I know we're not on the best of terms."

"No, we're not on *any* terms. Too much shit come with you, and I'm not with it no more."

"I made my mistakes, Angela, but I'm gettin' life together and I need you with me." He moved closer to her.

She stepped back.

"I see you need more time to yourself. I guess I should be leavin', huh?" He sat the box and the card down.

"Whatever." She noticed the new black drop-top CLK Benz sitting in the driveway when she opened the door.

He stepped out the door and turned to her. "I love you, Angela, no matter how hard you act. I know you still love me. See you soon."

She shut the door. *How the fuck he going to come around here unexpected and call me out on Christmas?* She walked in her room and got her purse. She needed something for her head, and her peoples definitely wa'n' allowing her to spark no weed. She locked her door and laid two lines out on the dresser. One up each nostril. "Goddamn!" She shook her head. This new shit was no joke—straight to the head. She was now ready for anything. She walked back to the family room, where her family was still chilling around the fireplace.

After the day got going she began wondering about Damien. She missed him. She got dressed in one of the pants suits her mother had given her. She was on her way out the door when she noticed Macs gift and cards. She unwrapped the box to reveal a long, red Anne Klein dress coat.

"My God, that's a beautiful coat," her mother said.

"It is nice, isn't it?" Angela almost felt bad about the way she treated him. She opened the card, and her mother watched the sadness come over her face as she read it.

I'm Sorry
Playing ball, running wild, no worries
Things a child should do.
Beatings, molestation, feeling insecure
Things that I went through
Family vacations, loving parents, nothing but love and affection.
Things I conceived in my mind
Poverty stricken projects, abusive father, making it on my own.
Why was my life so unkind
As frustrations were taken out on me.
Didn't they hear me say, I'm Sorry.

Now my childhood is gone and I stand as a man
Still facing the past everyday, the best I can
I never know what my future holds
Stay strong, get help, lean towards God
A strong black man chooses his destiny
These are all the things that I am told
No one knows how many times me and the problem has come
Face to face and all I've done is cried.
Strength comes from you and I have to have you in my life.
If I fail again, I want you to know that I have really tried.
Another mistake in life and again I have failed.

I say I regret it once and I say it again
Didn't you hear me say, I'm Sorry.

With much sincerity,
Love Mac

She passed the box and card to her mother, asking her to put it in the room, and walked out the door.

She arrived at Damien's house and strolled in with her gift in hand. "Heah, baby! Merry Christmas." She gave him a hug.

He seemed to force a smile.

She came in to find his brother and sister relaxing on the couches.

Damien began to open his gift. "Thank you, Angela. I really like this. I'm sorry I didn't pick you up anything, but I'm not a holiday person. Growing up, Christmas was just another day, and now I look at it the same way—just another day. For special ones in my life I show my love all year; I don't need a holiday."

"It's okay. I'm just so glad you're here and I have the opportunity to spend this day with you. That means everything." She leaned over and put her mouth on his ear and whispered, "The best gift is yet to come; you have to unwrap it upstairs."

"I'll see you all later." Damien took Angela's hand and walked upstairs. When he walked in the room he scooped her up.

She yelled as he slammed her to the bed and

crawled on top of her. She spent the majority of the day loving him.

The day passed quickly, and the evening, even faster. Damien was asleep and was awakened by the sweet kisses and touches of his love. "Happy birthday, baby." Angela stroked her hand up and down his back.

He lay there motionless as if he was still asleep, enjoying the soft, sensuous touch of his lover. Nothing in the world ever felt so good and made him totally relax to a state that nothing mattered. Today was his birthday, and to him, his birthday meant more than Christmas.

"I hope you didn't make plans for today," Angela said, "because I have the day already planned out, from breakfast to breakfast."

Damien knew that he had made other engagements, but if she wanted to celebrate his birthday with him in some laid back, unforgettable kind of way, then so be it. He was hers from breakfast to breakfast. He turned over on his back. "So what's the plan?"

She moved in closer, laying her head on his chest and her hand on his stomach. "We're going to start the day making love to each other, then breakfast will follow. Catch an early movie, then we will go to an undisclosed place. And that's where we'll be until breakfast time tomorrow. Can I have the entire day?" She began to kiss his neck and chest.

"I did have a few things to do," he said real slow.

"Is that right?" She ran her tongue slowly across his nipples. She could feel him starting to get aroused. She reached out and took him into her hand and stroked him gently again. "I can't be with you all day?"

"Ummmmmmmm, Angela," was his only response.

She climbed on top of him and guided him inside her. He let out a sigh of satisfaction, and they began to fuck like crazed animals for five minutes.

Then his body began to shake, and he squeezed her to him so tight, her breath was taken away. She started to get up.

"Don't move, don't move."

"You still leavin' me today?" she asked, relaxing in his arms.

"Actually, I have to run to Carolina, but you can ride with me."

She began to smile. That was all she wanted to hear, even if they did nothing. As long as she was with him.

After a quick shower and breakfast, they were on their way. Damien had asked Angela to drive while he lay back, relaxed, and rolled blunts while traveling down 85 South headed to Durham, NC.

They arrived at the home of one of his colleagues. She kind of figured he was in the business also when she saw the phat-ass Acura that sat in front of the condo, sitting on dubs.

Damien pulled the 9mm out from under the mat, put one in the chamber, and slid it into the Chanel purse he had picked up for her in DC.

She looked at him confused.

"It won't be needed, but it's better to have it and not need it than to need it and not have it."

They got out the car. She pulled her bag on her

shoulder and watched as he slid on his Avirex jacket that matched his jeans. She knew her man was on and was turned on by just being with him.

As they went inside the condo, a tall, light-skinned guy with curly hair showed Damien mad love. He stood about 6' 3" and was very muscular. She sat down as the two men went into the kitchen. From her vantage point she could see the money and coke being pulled from the cabinets. This made her nervous, but at the same time, it was exciting her.

Moments later she and Damien were out the door headed to another associate's house. When they arrived, Angela's mouth dropped at the sight of the man's beautiful home. The older gentle-man stood in front in a Dickies jumpsuit. She realized that one of the arms to the jumpsuit was just hanging. She was curious about what led to him losing his arm. He stood about six feet with a very large frame. I'm talkin' 300 pounds easily. The older gentleman's head was full of grey, and his beard held the same color. It was thick and neatly trimmed and had a very distinguished look.

"What happen to his arm?"

"Long time ago in New York, he was part of the 1940's heroin epidemic in Harlem. Some say he owed money, some say he had skimmed off the top, but they took a bat and beat his right hand and arm so bad, it had to be amputated. He's gotten along good over the years without it." Damien took the gun out of her purse and placed it back under the seat. He pulled the bag from the back, and they headed to the porch where the older gentleman was standing.

"What you say, young 'un? Look like you in

good spirits and seem to be doin' well. Who's this beautiful lady?"

"This is Angela."

The older gentleman hugged Angela around her neck. "Come on in, young 'un."

They went into the living room and took a seat on the antique furniture. A woman who appeared to be in her forties came in. Her hair had silver streaks in it, which convinced Angela that she was at least in her fifties, but her style was that of class and elegance.

"Heah, Daddy, can I get you and your guest anything?"

Damien quickly jumped up and hugged the lady when he noticed her presence. "Hello, Aunt Mable."

"Good to see you, Buttons," she said to Damien. "You really have to come and visit more often."

"Yes, ma'am. I try, but the store keep me so busy. I'm trying to build a base so I can live like Uncle John in my later years." Damien pointed to his close friend. Because of their age and the respect he had gained for John over the years, he gave them titles. Calling them by their first name wasn't for him; he wasn't old enough.

"Put business first and your future will fall into place, Buttons. Remember that," she said walking off.

"Take this, Mommy." John handed her the bag Damien had given him.

"So how long you here for, young 'un?" John asked Damien.

"On my way out now." Damien stood up. "It's my birthday and she made plans, so I'm heading on back to VA."

They walked outside to the car. Damien stopped and stared at John's new deep burgundy Cadillac Deville with the leather white interior and chrome Cadillac rims on which the Vogues sat.

"Uncle John, if you ever get rid of this, I got first dibs."

"I keep that in mind, young 'un." John smiled and showed his gold crowns.

Then they got in the truck and made their way. "They seem like nice peoples, Buttons," Angela said smiling as she drove away.

"The best. I want my life to fall just like his. Aunt Mable and Uncle John been together since they were in high school. Now they're in their fifties and still going strong. He's an old hustler, but now he has stores, real estate, and own an afterhours club in Raleigh; he's pretty much straight for life. They've traveled all over the world, and I really doubt if he wants for anything."

"Do they have kids?"

"Yeah, he has a daughter in California. She's an air traffic controller. She went to Hampton too." Damien smiled, thinking about the coincidence.

"Really?"

"His son went to Morgan State in Baltimore. Uncle John was paying his tuition, rent, and sending him dough to live, and that niggah was fuckin' with that shit. So Uncle John cut his ass off. He decided to stay up there. Far as I know he still up there strung out on heroin."

"Damn! Some just don't realize how good they have it."

"Yeah, they really don't." Damien stared at Angela and smiled.

"What?"

"You know what? You got it the same fuckin' way."

"My parents ain't got money like his."

"Yeah, but they doin' all right. They pay your tuition, and they pay your rent. What?"

"And I plan on takin' advantage of it like I'm doin'—I ain't gonna fuck it up."

"I'm gonna hold you to that shit. You can believe that, baby!"

The early movie was out by the time they arrived at Columbus Theaters in the downtown Virginia Beach area. The matinee had already started, so Angela talked him into going to Barnes and Noble and having a cappuccino until the next show began. He wasn't crazy about it, but this was her thing—she'd planned this day, and he was going to allow her to guide him through it.

They went inside, and she picked up the *Cycle* magazine because of his love for motorcycles. She got herself an *Essence*, a table, and two cups of cappuccino. After looking through the magazine, Angela could tell Damien was getting restless. Then she remembered a magazine that she'd seen at Mac's house. She went over to the shelf and brought back the *Robb Report*. He began to look through it. Moments later, when she glanced over at him, the magazine had his full attention. When it was time to go Damien brought the *Robb Report*. He had already filled out the card for a subscription.

After the movie they ran by her condo and retrieved her night bag. When they arrived at the Virginia Beach Resort, Angela had already made reservations for the room and dinner at the four-

star restaurant inside the resort, Tradewinds. Tradewinds gave them an astonishing view of the
Chesapeake Bay and the relaxing mood of an
ocean front café.

Dinner was fit for a king and the atmosphere of
candlelight and soft music set the mood for what
was to come. After a few drinks, they made it back
to the room. While Damien stood on the balcony
collecting his thoughts, Angela was in the bathroom running water for his bath. She asked him to
undress and come into the bathroom. He sat there
wondering what would make a woman treat him in
such a way. He knew money was what kept most
women going, but it was more than that. The style
and money may have gotten her attention, but it
wasn't money that was keeping her there, making
her do the things she did and treat him as if he was
the most important thing in the world.

Angela, young and outgoing, was learning fast.
She'd met many girls at Hampton and, listening to
girl talk, realized that a woman handled her business like a lady but also took care of her man. She
knew making him feel like he was her world would
either make him take advantage of her or give
back and show her the same love. Damien showed
her the same love, and it brought the best out of
her.

She took the cloth and went over his body,
bathing him slowly and thoroughly. He leaned
back and enjoyed every second, thinking that no
man had a love like his. After drying him off and
applying lotion to his body, she went to her bag
and pulled out a pair of silk boxers with Christmas
designs. Then she escorted him to the couch, removed an already rolled blunt from her purse, and

lit it. She passed it to him and excused herself to the bathroom. Minutes later, which felt like an eternity to Damien, she returned wearing a short white silk see-through robe. Damien's eyes widened as she allowed the robe to drop and reveal the most perfectly shaped body in a white thong with little elves and Santas on it, with a matching bra.

When he noticed the new tattoo Angela had gotten—she had a set of tiger paws going up her leg that ended at her kitty cat—his hormones took off. He stood up and picked her up. She wrapped her legs around him, and they fell on top of the bed. The embrace lasted till morning.

The knock at the door woke the two, and Damien opened the door to retrieve the room service that Angela had filled out and put on the door. He uncovered the food and looked over at his girl. *She is incredible.* All he needed for his life to be complete. He pictured Uncle John and Aunt Mable, then himself and Angela. A smile came across his face; he felt something he had never felt. *This shit here is real.*

"Angela, get the phone," Monica yelled from her bedroom.

Angela didn't respond.

Monica got up and went to her room and opened the door, but she wasn't there. Then she heard noise in the bathroom. "Angela."

"What, girl?"

"Get the phone; you know I have company. You need to get the phone or turn the ringer off."

"Stop cryin' all the fuckin' time."

"Just get the phone." Monica left out of her room.

Angela rushed to the phone, thinking it was Damien in New York for the weekend. "Hello," she said in an excited tone.

"How are you today?"

"I'm fine, Mac. How are you?" she asked in a nonchalant manner.

"Were you expecting someone else?"

"I was in the shower. You're going to have to let me call you back."

"We haven't talked since Christmas, and I figured you would of call by now. How did you like the gift?"

"It was nice, but I don't want you buyin' me anything else. Matter a fact, I really can't accept it."

"Well, I gave it to you from the heart, so I can't take it back. Angela, you don't seem to understand—I'm not and I can't let you go. I love you."

She hung up the phone. The more she pushed him away, the more aggressive he was becoming. The phone rang again. She picked it up quickly and answered with an attitude. "Hello." Her tone was loud and forceful.

"Who you talkin' to? That's not the way you answer the phone."

"I'm sorry. I thought you were my moms callin' again."

"You all right this morning?"

"Yeah, I'm okay. Now I'm really okay," she said with a smile in her voice.

He smiled too. "Are you?"

"I'm gettin' so attached to you, Damien. When

you're here I want to be with you, and if you aren't I'm missin' you to no end."

"I can relate, baby, but you realize that business has to be taken care of if I plan any future for me and you, right?"

"Yes." Then the phone beeped. "Hold on, please."

"Yes," she answered with attitude.

"Don't hang up on me, Angela."

"I'm on the other line."

"Fuck that! I know it ain't that young-ass punk," he yelled.

She clicked back over to finish talking to Damien. Her good mood jumped back up when she realized he would be home New Year's Eve, but she knew it was time to handle Mac, who was really getting out of hand.

Angela came into the living room with Quinn and Monica. "I'm going to call the police because Mac keep trippin' and I can't take it, Monica."

"Well, Monday morning we'll go downtown and let them know. That's one niggah you could have left alone," Monica said, "but we'll handle it."

"Where your friend, Angela?" Quinn asked.

Angela remembered that Damien told her never tell anyone about his whereabouts and when he leaves out of town. "He's in DC."

"See Quinn's new car?" Monica asked.

"Little somethin'-somethin'." Quinn smiled and put on his Ralph Lauren black leather jacket to go with his black Lugz.

"Leavin' already?"

"Yeah, I have to get back to Petersburg; I got mad shit to take care of up there."

They walked outside. Angela was surprised to see his new black 325 BMW. "Damn, Quinn! This

shit is nice." Angela looked at Monica, who was
smiling ear to ear. Her man was rising on the social
ladder. He was turning into one of those guys that
she had always admired and now she had one of
her own. She was so glad she got Rome to put her
man on and was proud of Quinn. And despite all
of her unfaithful actions, she really loved him.

Quinn pulled in the Hampton Club complex.
This stop was mandatory before going back to
Petersburg. He walked up to Rome's apartment
and was invited in. Quinn noticed the dark-skinned
guy sitting in the chair smoking a blunt. Quinn
spoke, but the guy gave no response. Rome had
walked to the back bedroom and reached deep inside the mattress and pulled out a whole brick all
ready cooked for Quinn. Quinn placed it in a
Food Lion bag, stuck it in his pants, and they all
walked out.

Rome and Quinn were talking as the stout,
dark-skinned guy followed. Quinn signaled for
shorty in the passenger side to get in the driver's
seat. As she got out and walked around to the driver
side Rome stared in amazement—he didn't think
Quinn had it in him.

"Damn, niggah! I like that."

"She's nice, right? She got three roommates.
They all live in a big-ass house in Petersburg right
off campus. And, son, all them bitches bad."

Rome was still staring into the girl's eyes. She
wore no makeup, but she was the finest dark-
brown shorty he'd ever seen. Her coal-black, wavy
hair was just slightly darker than her skin, but she
filled the jeans with the widest hips and phattest

ass he'd ever seen. All he could do was rub his dick off this one. "I'd pay for some that ass, son." He knew Monica was Quinn's girl and wanting this bitch was no disrespect since she was just something on the side. And far as Rome was concerned, there was no better way to play.

"Y'all niggahs need to get up to Petersburg. It's like that all day. Holla at a niggah." Quinn gave Rome a pound.

Rome and his new partner got in the GS300 and drove off. They'd been talking. This guy was trying to get Rome down with him. The kid was in his junior year at Hampton University, from Philly. Him and his peoples had a lucrative business bringing bricks into Hampton and Newport News.

Rome noticed Sincere on campus, first fucking with cute bitches, then fucking with niggahs with phat whips. He wasn't flashy—jeans, hoody, and Timbs was his normal attire. One of the girls that Sincere had been fucking started liking Rome. Sincere didn't care; it was his way of meeting another baller. It wasn't many cats who had it like Rome did, so he felt good to hang with a niggah who had what he had. It felt good fucking with new niggahs, meeting new bitches, and balling out of control.

One day he even asked Rome to get down with him and his peoples, but Rome let him know that he only fucked around with the cats he'd been dealing with forever, but he was still cool and if anything changed . . .

Rome dropped Sincere off and headed to Norfolk. This felt like a night for clubbing, but not by himself. He swung by Angela and Monica's condo to see what they were up to. "Sound like a

Pazzazz night to me. What's up?" he said, entering
the condo.

"You got us?" Monica asked.

"Why bitches always yellin' that shit. I know y'all
got money."

"Not the point," Angela told him. "You heard
my girl—do you got us?"

"Yeah, but y'all got to meet me. I'll call before I
leave my house." Rome sat down and rolled the
blunt.

Monica handed him a small bag containing a
couple grams of coke. He sprinkled some onto the
weed and rolled it. The "yes-yes" had their eyes
bloodshot red. They kicked for a few until Rome
had to leave and catch Kappatal Kuts before going
out.

Angela pulled on Granby St. The line was
around the building with no parking anywhere in
sight. "I am not parkin' in no garage tonight."

"There's Rome talkin' to some niggah."

They pulled over, and to their surprise, the
dude was about to pull off. Angela lucked up and
got a close spot.

They kicked it for a moment until Sincere
strolled up. He knew security; he showed a little
love, and they all walked inside, still having to pay,
but without waiting in line.

Sincere walked to bar on the first floor. He signaled to the bartender that Rome and the ladies
were with him, and four glasses appeared on the
bar, filled with shots of Rémy. The four made their
way past the laughter of the Comedy Club on the
second floor and found a table on the third.

"Thank you," Monica said.

"My pleasure, shorty," Sincere said. And to the waitress who made her way to the table, "Cristal and four glasses."

The girls looked at each other as if to ask, "Who is Rome's new friend?"

"Damn! My fault. Sincere, this is Monica and Angela, my sisters. This is my man, Sincere." Monica and Angela glanced but tried not to stare. But this dark-ass niggah, rockin' braids that some bitch had freaked for him, had the girls wondering who this niggah was, showing them mad love.

They began to talk and conversate, but kept getting interrupted by the different ballers and players coming up showing what some would consider love. But it actually was respect to Sincere. Rome was curious because he knew his status could blow, hanging with a ghetto celeb.

Monica and Angela just liked the attention they were receiving from the onlookers, standing around watching the waitress pop the champagne and pour four glasses, and then sit the rest on ice.

Suddenly two girls came speeding to the table, followed by another pair. Sincere stood up and received a bundle of hugs. "Yo, Rome, this is Kay-Kay and Reva, my sisters from the crib.

"And this is Seri and Star," Reva said. "They from the spot too."

"Germantown 'ho's up in here," Sincere joked.

"You don't know, better ask somebody," Kay-Kay said smiling.

"So what's goin' on at Norfolk State, ladies? Why don't I buy you all a drink and y'all tell me how things are going."

They walked over to the bar, with Sincere leading the way and his arm around Seri, as the other three followed. Seri was light—what you call yellow. She had light-brown hair and was a real pleasure to look at. Not to mention, her 40DD's pushed up for the world to see, but not at all trashy . . . in no way.

"Goddamn, Kay-Kay," Rome said loud enough for only Angela and Monica to hear as they sat at the table with their eyes on Sincere and the Philly girls.

"Go get her, player," Angela said.

"He scared. Niggah don't want no pussy, An." They both started laughing.

"No rush. No rush," was all Rome said as he watched Kay-Kay's ass swing side to side in the snug-fitting polyester pants. The tight-fitting shirt with buttons only at the top revealed her pierced belly button and hairline, which gave him an instant hard on.

They saw no more of them until the club ended. As Rome walked with Angela and Monica to the parking lot, Sincere came up behind them, "Ladies, it was nice meeting you both. I hope we see each other again.

"Yo, Rome," Kay-Kay said "what's up. She wants some breakfast—I got Seri—come on, niggah."

"Shit . . . niggah, you know I'm down. Let's go." Rome turned and said his good-byes to Angela and Monica and burst. He had to see what the young Philly girl was 'bout it.

After leaving IHOP, Sincere and Rome took the girls back to their house in Merrimac Landing, where the four young ladies shared a four-bedroom home. After thirty minutes of blunts and more conversation, Rome and Karen retired to her room.

By the time morning came, Karen felt she had a new man, and Rome would tell her no different. The young girl from Philly had him open with her style and graceful movements, and having that bomb-ass body and the skills to go along definitely didn't hurt.

Chapter Eighteen

Angela felt like a weight was taken off her shoulder when she left the courthouse. The court told Mac to stay away. Now, she had taken another restraining order out against him. *Once papers were served, he would be out of her life for sure.*

"How can somebody so fine be so fucked up?"

"It goes back to that niggah childhood. He says the way he was brought up and his household did it to him and that what makes him act the fool sometimes. I feel sorry for him, but I can't take care of a grown-ass man, you know what I mean?"

"Shit! I know, girl, but we learn from all our mistakes. All of them."

"Well, we made enough for '96, and all we can do is pray that '97 brings about a change for the better."

"It will, starting tomorrow when your man gets back. What we gonna do tomorrow night anyway to bring in the New Year?"

"Whatever. Long as I'm with my baby." Angela smiled.

* * *

Just as Angela was thinking of Damien in New York, he was doing the same as he explored the diamond district. He didn't get her anything for Christmas, but after all the love she'd shown him, he had to let her know it wasn't in vain. He knew he had never had a female express herself the way Angela did, and he never wanted to see himself without her.

After meeting with JB and finding out that things were real good on the business end and his future was in no jeopardy, he went out to find her a little something. While riding through Manhattan, he pulled down his sun visor and the two pictures of Angela fell in his lap. He knew he had a beautiful girl, a very precious jewel that any man would be glad to have on his arm.

He studied one from head to toe, from the fly cut she wore, to the sexy Donna Karan sandals. The second picture was more recent—he was standing there, looking like the Big Willie he was, as she leaned into his arms, her arm around him and her left hand resting on his chest. He imagined the soft touch of her hands and the way she took the beautiful, freshly airbrushed nails and lightly ran them down his back as he made love to her. "Wow! Goddamn, girl," he said out loud to himself.

He went into the district to find her a ring. Something to say, "I love you, and I'm not going nowhere." He put the pictures back above the sun visor. He knew he would need some help, so he scooped his sister Rhonda, who had the taste to help him pick out the perfect ring.

* * *

Angela pulled in front of Monica's house. "I'll be back in about an hour; I'm going to my peoples' house."

"You gonna tell your moms?"

"Yeah, I really think I need to now; plus, I want her to meet Damien tomorrow—that's who I'm goin' into the New Year with, and he's going to be a permanent part of my life. It's time she met him. Monica, don't forget to page Rome and see if he has some candy, and you know we need some weed.

"You got money?"

"I told you to call, didn't I?" Angela pulled off.

Angela walked into the house to find her mother packing her lunch for her 3 to 11 shift. "Heah, Ma."

"What you doin' today, Angela? Surprise to see you. I saw Ray's mother at Farm Fresh. She said that you can still give her a call."

"All right."

"Where you comin' from?"

"I had to get a restraining order against Mac."

"What?" Her mother stopped what she was doing.

"That's why I wasn't tryin' to see him Christmas. He decided he wanted to hit and control me. When he first did it, I cut him loose.

"Lately I've been talkin' to this guy, Damien, and one day Mac come to my job and tried to do the same thing, but Damien was there to straighten it out. I really care for Damien, Mom, but Mac won't leave me alone. So I went to the courts today."

"What the police say?"

"They're goin' to serve him the papers, and then if he comes near me, he'll be picked up."

"You be careful, baby; some men are really crazy—I mean really crazy. Why are you just telling me this? I want you to start sharing things with me; I am your mother. Okay?"

"You're right, Ma."

"So when I'm going to meet this Damien character?"

"Tomorrow I'm going to stop by." They hugged and left out the house together.

Angela picked up Monica, and they were on their way to Fat Joe's house, where him and Rome were chilling, smoking, looking at "Rap City."

Afterwards, the girls headed back to their condo to waste the rest of the day on another level. The ringing of the phone in the late hour woke the young ladies up. It was Quinn in the car, telling Monica to open the door. The girls had passed out and left the television watching them.

Quinn's knock at the door was Angela's good night signal. She went in her room and paged Damien. He never called back, but she never knew it. She was dead to the world.

The following afternoon, New Year's Eve, Monica and Angela were still in the bed. The loud bass from Rome's Lexus brought Angela to her feet, thinking it was Damien, but she knew by the rattling of the car it wasn't him. *His truck didn't rat-*

tle. The knock at the door had her questioning herself. She ran to it, and to her surprise it was just Rome and Fat Joe coming up the stairs.

She quickly ran in her room to put a robe over the oversized number 23 Bulls jersey she had on. It revealed a little too much. (It was Damien's and reeked of his Curve cologne; the reason she wore it.)

"I thought y'all were Damien. Need to get all that rattlin' fixed—shit don't sound good."

"Fuck you talkin'?" Rome ignored her comment. "Hell y'all doin' tonight?"

"We talkin' about gettin' two bitches and goin' out Waterside and checkin' out the fireworks."

Angela yelled out in the direction of Monica's room. "We goin' out Waterside tonight?"

"Down for whatever."

Rome asked, "Who here with her? Quinn?"

"Yeah. But I have to see what Damien has planned; I'm sure he's down."

"We headin' to the mall to pick up some shit," Joe said. "What you gonna do?"

"I'm chillin', waitin' on my man."

Rome asked her, "You always play fair like that?"

"I do . . . when my man play fair with me." Angela had a devious smile. "Which mall y'all goin' to anyway?"

"Coliseum," Rome told her. "Bring yo' ass. I got you on a T-shirt or something, if you help me pick out something nice for my new babe."

They jumped in the whip and began roaming. They started at Coliseum and ended up at

Chesapeake Square. By the time they dropped Angela off it was dark, and she was wondering why she hadn't heard from Damien.

She showered and changed. The plan was to meet Fat Joe, his friend, Rome, and KayKay down by the Bank of America building downtown. Just as the clock struck ten, Angela began to worry.

"If he don't show, just swing with me and Quinn."

"Thanks, Monica, but I ain't tryin' to be the third wheel. Y'all go ahead. If he comes, I'll meet you'll down there."

"You sure; you know it's not a problem?" Quinn asked.

"I know. But tonight I want to wait on him."

When they left Angela lit a blunt and put in a CD, Tupac's *Me Against the World.* She listened to the lyrics and realized for the first time why this man was a legend and why her man also was a thug for life.

As time slowly crept away she realized he wasn't going to make it. But she understood he was a busy man and, the way he lived, anything could come up. She had gotten a bottle of J. Rogét for her and Damien to pop open for the New Year. She got the bottle and sat on the couch. Just as she was beginning to accept the disappointment and prepare for a night of loneliness, she could feel her body tremble from bass. Then the sounds began to become clearer. She jumped up and ran to the door. As she opened the door, she saw the new butter Timbs, untied and the tag still dangling, hit the top step. By the time his body hit the doorway, she was in his arms, full of joy.

He squeezed her—she knew he'd missed her by

the way he'd taken her breath with his embrace—
and they shared a very passionate kiss.

She stared into his eyes with the biggest smile.
She looked down at her watch and saw it read only
11:15. "Can we go to Waterside?"

"It's on you; I'm with you."

She really wanted to be with her crew, but fine
as her man was looking, she almost said, "Let's just
stay the fuck in."

"You look cute, baby." Damien admired her
DKNY jeans, Nine West boots, and the leather
he'd gotten her.

She knew his style was thuggish and she liked it.
So when they walked to truck she never com-
mented on his camouflaged suit, new Timbs, and
Phat Farm T-shirt that was set off by the iced-down
medallion swinging from his neck. Instead she just
admired him for him. *Fuck the occasion.*

They headed downtown. Damien felt this would
be the perfect time to give her the ring . . . as soon
as the fireworks go off.

They joined Angela's friends. Everybody was
standing in the cold, bouncing around, trying to
stay warm as the skies roared and lit up from the
fireworks. They all popped champagne and
hugged their significant others.

Damien reached down in his side cargo pocket.

She smiled a big smile when he pulled the 3ct
diamond solitaire from the box and placed it on
her ring finger.

"This is to say that I promise never to leave you
and that we are a team until the end."

Angela eyes began to water. She never knew she
meant that much to him.

He leaned over and hugged her tight. "I love you, Angela. That, I promise you, will never change."

Angela was shocked to hear those words. She just squeezed him harder and cherished the moment.

After an hour of celebrating and gulping down champagne, everyone went their separate ways. Angela and Damien ended up back at the condo with Monica and Quinn. They decided to play a few hands of spades until the early morning before retiring to their rooms.

After intense lovemaking, they fell asleep, snuggled and cuddled in the each other's arms.

Angela had heard the phone ring earlier that morning, and the noise from Monica and Quinn in the living room didn't allow her to go back to sleep. She walked out into the living room, while Damien was getting dressed. "What's up, girl?"

"Nothin' at all. Mac called here three times demandin' to talk to you."

"Fuck him! He need to carry his ass and get a life. Tell me this—how can a man as fine as him and with the money he has turn into straight bitch?"

"Angela, you really need to be careful because the way he acted on the phone and his past actions really shows me that he is disturbed."

"You right, but I think he has too much to lose to do anything crazy crazy; plus, I'm not intimidated by him no more."

Damien came out the room and put on his coat, and Quinn grabbed his, knowing it was his chance to burst. They walked out and went to the

LX450 and BMW parked beside each other, neither noticing the drop-top Benz parked across the street.

Damien opened his truck door and heard a voice behind him say, "Who's Big Willie now, muthafucka?"

Three shots rang out, and Quinn tried to jump in the beamer.

Angela and Monica heard two more shots. They ran to the door and ran outside. As they ran down the stairs in time to see Mac's black Mercedes speeding out the parking lot and onto Ocean View Avenue.

Both girls ran to their man's side, screaming hysterically.

"Somebody, call 911," Monica yelled as she took Quinn's hand. "Hurry up!"

Quinn lay motionless on the front seat of his car with a gunshot wound to his chest and his stomach.

Angela stood there crying out of control.

Neighbors came out to see what was going on. Angela looked down at Damien lying in the puddle of blood that turned his army fatigues and Phat Farm shirt into a bloody mess.

Norfolk police was quick to arrive, along with the ambulance and rescue squads. They moved Monica and Angela out the way, and the girls sat on the curb, comforting each other. They watched as they took Quinn out the car and placed him in the ambulance. Monica got in and rode to the hospital with him—he wasn't moving but was still alive.

Angela stood watching as they placed a white sheet over Damien's body. Her entire body began to shake, and her legs gave away. She sat balled up on the wall as the detectives approached her to take a statement. She let them know it was Mac.

Afterwards, she went inside to call Noriega. It was the only number she had for anybody in his family.

A little later, the phone rang. Monica was crying to a point you couldn't understand anything she was saying. "Slow down, Monica . . . please."

"He's dead. He died in the operating room," Monica said through her cries.

"I'm on my way."

Angela got her keys and rushed to Norfolk General.

As the clock struck twelve New Year's night, Angela and Monica rested on the couch in complete silence. All you could hear was the whistling of the cold wind blowing in off the Chesapeake Bay. Monica was staring into space with a blank look on her face, and Angela couldn't stop the tears from flowing. She just wanted to sit and drown her sorrows in the leftover champagne and snort the coke that they had stashed away.

Monica's grandmother and Angela's parents had come over to persuade the girls to come home, but they knew they had to deal with the situation themselves and needed each other, not anybody who wanted to point fingers and ask a lot of questions.

The knock at the door scared both girls. They jumped up instantly, staring at each other to see who was going to answer.

Monica eased to the door and peeked out. It

was Noriega and two of his soldiers. When he walked in they both hugged him as if they never wanted to let him go. They stepped back, and Angela burst into tears.

Noriega stood there in his camouflage outfit, new butter Timbs, and an Azzure T-shirt, a long chain hanging down to his stomach. "So did they get the kid?"

"Yeah," Angela told him. "They went to his house and never found the weapon. He probably threw it in the Bay when he drove over the Hampton Bridge."

"A'ight. That means he's comin' out on bail." Noriega looked at Angela. "I need you to show us where he lives, okay."

"Time to show these VA niggahs how we get down in Crooklyn," one of the soldiers said.

They rode out for her to show him where he lived and then got a ride back home.

Next time she heard, Noriega had gone back to New York to help out with his cousin's funeral arrangements. Damien's funeral was being held on Saturday at Woodward Thompson Chapel on One Troy Avenue, Brooklyn, and Quinn's was being held on Sunday at Fitchett Funeral Home on Liberty Street in the South Norfolk area.

Meanwhile Mac was released on $50,000 bond. Police thought everything was drug related and didn't put any emphasis on the case.

Angela and Monica left Friday night for New York. When they arrived there, she was surprised not to see Noriega.

Saturday came and the funeral was harder than the girls expected. Angela took it harder than some of Damien's own family, but Noriega showed up to help pull her together.

After the funeral they all met at Damien's mother's house. As Angela approached the home, Rhonda dropped her plate and grabbed Angela and slammed her to the car.

Monica grabbed Rhonda, and Kim slapped the shit out of her, yelling, "Get your fuckin' hands off her."

"I told you, bitch. I told you don't fuck my brother up," Rhonda yelled between cries. "Why? I told you." And she fell to the ground, losing her breath and screaming.

Kim held Rhonda, trying to comfort her as the tears streamed down both their faces.

When the girls climbed into the car to leave, Noriega walked over and hugged Monica. "You be strong, baby, and everything will come together. I'll be callin' to check on you soon."

Then he eased over to Angela and stared into her eyes. She didn't know what to say or do; her eyes watered as they embraced. A tear fell from his eyes, as many began to flow from hers. "Look, my cousin had mad love for you. Don't allow the circumstances to fuck up your life. Keep your head up and keep going. If you need anything, don't hesitate to call. Be strong and put it behind you— it's over. Revenge is the sweetest thing in the fuckin' world," he said with a smirk.

Angela just stared, knowing what he meant.

* * *

They arrived back in Norfolk with just enough time to change and get over to Quinn's "set up." When they pulled in front of the house and made their way to the door, they caught looks as if they were the ones who murdered him. Upon entering the house, his mother embraced Monica showing her love. His father never spoke, he just turned and walked away.

Quinn's brother just stared with hatred in his eyes before all hell broke loose. "My brother lost his muthafuckin' life over y'all—simple-ass bitches!—and you got the audacity to show up at my mama house. All this fucked up shit in the world and he loses his life behind some nasty-ass 'ho's." His eyes filled with tears.

"Shut your mouth and go in the room, Aaron," his mother said.

Aaron had only said out loud what everybody else was thinking.

"Monica, honey," she continued, "I know things weren't your fault, but you know how brothers and family who don't have God in their life can react. I'm sorry." She touched Monica's hand.

"I just wanted to come by and give my condolences. I'm sorry for what you have to go through. I really am. I'm going to leave, though; I don't want to build anymore tension than I already have." Monica hugged her again and made her exit.

As she was leaving, Rome, Ski, and Fat Joe came up. "Y'all a'ight?" Fat Joe asked.

"We will be as soon as they lock that simple muthafucka up," Angela said.

Rome told her, "Ya musta just got back."

"Yeah. About an hour ago."

The guys began to smirk. They were surprised the girls hadn't heard. "Locked up?! That kid who shot Quinn and your boy is dead."

"What you talkin' about?" Angela asked.

"They found the guy burned to death in his drop-top Benz. On the news they said he'd been shot twice, then his car was soaked down with gasoline inside and out, then torched. He was burned beyond recognition."

Monica and Angela looked at each other. They both knew Noriega had handled that shit like a real niggah—A LIFE FOR A LIFE.